MONTANA MAVERICKS

Welcome to Big Sky Country! Where spirited men and women discover love on the range.

HIDDEN GEMS RANCH

As the seasons change in the small town of Tenacity, Montana, so does opportunity. The high school football team has a shot at a winning season, and with fall pumpkin festivals, Christmas events and the discovery of precious kimberlite, the town is buzzing. For some cowboys and cowgirls, though, the prize they most value seems just out of reach. Could love be the ultimate gem discovered in Tenacity?

THE MAVERICK'S HOMECOMING

After a career-ending injury, former pro footballer Finn Monahan is back home in Tenacity to revive the high school's struggling football team. But coming home also revives old feelings for his first love, Kenzie Osborne. Rumors whisper that Kenzie is newly divorced...and pregnant. Could Kenzie be Finn's true endgame?

Dear Reader,

Former hometown hero and NFL quarterback Finn Monahan has just returned to Tenacity. He's doing a brisk business selling real estate to the new residents of Tenacity who were attracted by the town's change of fortunes. And he's also allowed himself to be talked into coaching Tenacity High's struggling football team.

Right away, he runs into his first love, school nurse Kenzie Osborne. Kenzie is newly divorced and as beautiful as ever—and not the least interested in rekindling an old flame. Her life is changing in a big way and the last thing she needs is to get too close to the first guy who broke her tender heart.

I hope this reunion story reminds you that love really can conquer all. And that the seeds of hope and prosperity have been known to take root even in the toughest times.

Happy reading, everyone,

Christine

THE MAVERICK'S HOMECOMING

CHRISTINE RIMMER

MONTANA MAVERICKS

Special thanks and acknowledgment are given to Christine Rimmer for her contribution to the Montana Mavericks: Hidden Gems Ranch miniseries.

Recycling programs for this product may not exist in your area.

ISBN-13: 978-1-335-14362-4

The Maverick's Homecoming

For questions and comments about the quality of this book, please contact us at CustomerService@Harlequin.com.

Harlequin Enterprises ULC
22 Adelaide St. West, 41st Floor
Toronto, Ontario M5H 4E3, Canada
www.Harlequin.com

HarperCollins Publishers
Macken House, 39/40 Mayor Street Upper,
Dublin 1, D01 C9W8, Ireland
www.HarperCollins.com

Printed in Lithuania

1 2 3 4 5 6 7 8 9 10 LIT 28 27 26 25

Christine Rimmer came to her profession the long way around. She tried everything from acting to teaching to telephone sales. Now she's finally found work that suits her perfectly. She insists she never had a problem keeping a job—she was merely gaining "life experience" for her future as a novelist. Christine lives with her family in Oregon. Visit her at christinerimmer.com.

Books by Christine Rimmer

Harlequin Special Edition

Montana Mavericks: Hidden Gems Ranch

The Maverick's Homecoming

Bravo Family Ties

Hometown Reunion
Her Best Friend's Wedding
Taking the Long Way Home
When Christmas Comes
His Best Friend's Girl
The Marriage Plan
A Secret Between Friends

Montana Mavericks: Behind Closed Doors

The Maverick's Dating Deal

Montana Mavericks: The Trail to Tenacity

Redeeming the Maverick

Visit the Author Profile page
at Harlequin.com for more titles.

Years ago when my children were much younger, we took them to the local Second Chance Animal Shelter where they each chose a kitten. Older son brought home a tiny black kitty and named him Tom. Younger son picked out a very active gray tabby he decided to call Ed. Tom and Ed are no longer with us, but they were the sweetest guys around. And I couldn't resist giving their names and personalities to the frisky kittens in this book. So this one's for you, Tom and Ed. I miss you both. Lots.

Prologue

Three and a half months ago

"Kenzie?" asked a deep voice from directly behind her. Kenzie Osborne knew that voice. Her stomach churning, she swiveled on the wooden barstool.

Yep. Finn Monahan.

Unbelievable. Almost fifteen years had rolled by since the day he broke her heart. That day, as he'd turned to walk away from her, she'd shouted that she hated him, that she would never speak to him again.

But life goes on. And remembering that painful afternoon now just made her feel even sadder than she had a moment before.

She stiffened her spine and put on a smile. "I heard you were back in town..." The words came out sounding strained, but not because of what had happened years ago. She had fresher heartaches to deal with now, heartaches that had nothing whatsoever to do with Finn.

Her stomach lurched again. She breathed in through her nose and ordered the uncomfortable feeling to pass as Finn's wide brow creased with a worried frown. "Look, Kenzie," he said. "The truth is, I followed you in here."

Here was the Grizzly Bar on Central Avenue in their hometown of Tenacity, Montana.

Why? she wondered sourly. What in the world could she and Finn Monahan possibly have to say to each other now?

Not a thing, that's what.

Drawing in another slow breath, she glanced around the knotty-pine-paneled space. All the tables were empty. Down at the end of the bar, a lone cowboy sat staring into a half-finished glass of beer. The bartender was nowhere to be seen.

And Finn just stood there, watching her. Apparently, he thought they had more to say to each other. "Honestly, Finn. I'm really not up for a trip down memory lane right now."

He looked at her with what actually seemed to be honest concern. "I'm not here to talk about old times, I promise you."

"Great," she said sincerely and then she waited for him to move along. He didn't. Instead, he remained right where he was and continued to stare at her with that worried look on his face. After several endless seconds of truly uncomfortable silence, she asked impatiently, "If not what happened years ago, then what *are* you here to talk about?"

"I saw you outside." He gestured back over his shoulder at the door to the street. "You seemed upset." He glanced at the crumpled papers she'd dropped on the bar and then went on, "You stopped out front and looked around like you weren't even sure where you were. I followed you in here because I just wanted to… Look. All you have to do is tell me. Are you okay?"

A weird squeak of laughter escaped her. She clapped a hand over her mouth to stifle the ridiculous sound. Laughing was a bad idea. Her emotions were all wonky. Laughter just might make her burst into tears.

And what had he asked her?

Right. *Are you okay?*

Why lie? He wanted to know what was wrong with her, fine. "Truthfully, Finn, I'm feeling a little low. My divorce is final." She grabbed the papers from the bar and shoved them at him. "I got these in the mail today. One look at them and I jumped in my car headed…" She drew in a slow breath through her nose. "Well, I'm not sure where I was headed. I found myself cruising along Central Avenue. About then, I decided that what I needed was a good, stiff drink… The rest you can probably figure out for yourself."

"Damn." Finn stared at the divorce decree in her outstretched hand and then met her eyes again. "Kenzie, I'm so sorry. I…" He swept off his Stetson and held it to his chest. "Hell. There has to be a right thing to say at this point. But I don't have a clue what that might be."

She shrugged. "Don't worry about it. The truth is that my marriage is toast and has been for a while now. Honestly, I'm trying really hard to move on."

"Well. Okay, then. That's good, right?" He asked the question carefully.

She sighed. "Yeah. It is good. But still. Getting the final papers is a real kick in the teeth, one that knocked the wind right out of me. It brought back the past seven years—eight, if you count the year my ex and I were dating…" She paused for another careful breath. Why was she still talking? Finn Monahan did not need to hear this.

And yet she kept right on. "It's just that, suddenly, I feel like I'm drowning, going under for the last time with no chance of rescue. You can't imagine all the hopes I once had, all the big dreams of love everlasting."

"Yeah, I can." He looked right in her eyes. She knew what he was thinking because she was thinking it, too. They'd been in love once, she and Finn. Yeah, they'd been teenagers then. But still. They'd shared big dreams and high hopes.

She dropped the decree on the bar again. "Sorry. I guess what I'm trying to say is that getting the final papers is no fun at all."

He seemed at a loss. "I can't even imagine."

"Never been married, huh?" Her question was rhetorical. She would have heard if the great Finn Monahan had ever taken the leap.

"Nope. Still single." At that moment, he almost looked shy.

So shoot her. She couldn't stop herself from thinking that her ex-high-school sweetheart had grown into a truly fine-looking man. He was bigger and broader than back in the day. And the faint beginnings of laugh lines and crow's feet? They only added character to his handsome face.

In high school, she had loved him with every fiber of her being. And then, when he left her, she'd hated him with the burning fury of a thousand suns. It had taken her a long time to get over him.

But all that was ancient history. Now, she had Tate to get over. The heartbreak she'd suffered when Finn walked away from her was water under a very old bridge.

She did find it somewhat disorienting, though, to have

him standing right here in front of her today of all days. She'd heard he was back in town. But this was the first time she'd seen him in person since he broke up with her all those years ago.

He seemed to be studying her face. Did she look as woozy as she felt? Was he waiting for her to do something alarming—perhaps pass out and fall off her stool? "You're pale," he said. "You sure you're—"

She cut him off with a weary wave of her hand. "Just a little queasy, that's all. It happened fast, my divorce. I get sick to my stomach just thinking about it."

Right then, the bartender emerged from the open doorway to the back room. He spotted Finn first and came straight for him. "What do you know?" He stuck out his beefy hand. "Finn Monahan, am I right?"

"That's right." The two men shook hands as Kenzie put all her energy into not being sick.

"I'm Dale Clutterbuck," the bartender said. "I moved to town eighteen years ago, which means I was here when you led the Tenacity Titans to back-to-back state championships. Then, twelve years ago now, I bought this bar from old Mr. Kelsy. Man, it's great that you've come back to town, Finn. And I do mean that sincerely. I heard you bought the Rawlings place. That's quite a house."

"Yeah. It's a beautiful property."

"It is indeed. You settling in alright?"

Finn slid a worried glance Kenzie's way. She squared her shoulders and managed a grim smile to signal that she was just fine.

His gaze swung back to Dale. "I'm doing well, Dale, thanks. I'm in real estate now and have been for a while. Things are looking up around here and I've got a feeling this town is going to do just fine in the future. As a matter of fact, I'm betting on Tenacity to come back big."

"Smart man," Dale replied with a firm nod. "Yeah, we've had some bad years. But that's over now. And you chose the right line of work. The real-estate market is only going to get hotter."

The bartender knew what he was talking about, Kenzie thought as she sucked in air, slowly and steadily, through her nose. The old days of political corruption were behind them. Tenacity's new mayor was trusted and admired by everyone in town. Money once stolen from the town coffers had been reclaimed at last. And then dinosaur bones had been discovered. The town had pulled together to build the Tenacity Dinosaur Center, which was now open and attracting tourists from all over.

Dale was still talking. "Well, don't be a stranger, Finn. It's real nice to have you back home." He turned to Kenzie then…and got his first good look at her. "Whoa!"

She tried a big smile. "Hey, Dale. Good to see you. How've you been?"

"I'm fine. But you don't look so good—it's Kenzie, am I right?" When she opened her mouth to tell him her last name, he put up a hand. "Wait, wait. Don't tell me. Hastings! Kenzie Hastings."

"School nurse, at your service." She tried a chuckle. Too bad it came out as more of a groan. "And it's Osborne. Kenzie Osborne. I, uh, recently took back my family name."

"Alright then, Kenzie Osborne." Dale leaned closer and asked gently, "Tell me the truth, now. You *sure* you're okay?"

Willing her stomach to settle the heck down, she took

off her denim jacket and hung it on the hook beneath the bar. "Must have been something I ate. But I'm feeling better now, honestly."

Finn caught her eye. "Ginger ale?"

She almost smiled. After all these years, he remembered. She used to crave ginger ale whenever she was feeling under the weather—which was often during the last couple of months they were together. "Ginger ale would be perfect, thank you."

"Coming right up. Finn?"

"Maker's Mark and ice."

"Done." Dale served their drinks and moved down the bar to get that lone cowboy another beer.

Finn sipped whiskey as Kenzie tackled her tall ginger ale. The fizzy drink helped. She grinned as she realized that Finn was still standing.

"Still haven't dared to sit down, huh?" she teased.

He looked pained. "Given our…history, it seemed like a good idea not to grab a seat until I'd been invited."

He had a point. But the past? It was forever ago. She patted the stool beside her. "Consider the hatchet officially buried."

He looked at her sideways. "There was a hatchet?"

"Come on." She gave the stool another tap. "Have a seat. Catch me up on the life of an NFL superstar."

Still, he hesitated to take the stool. "I wasn't a superstar for all that long." He eyed her with concern. "And you still look pale."

"I promise you, I'm fine. And you know what? If you're not in the mood to tell me what you've been up to, that's okay with me. Just sit down beside me and let me cry on your shoulder. I could use an old friend to talk to right now."

"A friend?" He smiled then, his real smile, the one that used to make her heart beat faster. "You mean that?" He sounded so young. And hopeful, too.

She smiled right back at him. "Stranger things have happened. Come on, it's been years. I'd say it's time to let the past go."

Finn took the stool. "Okay, Kenzie. Talk."

Why not? she thought. He was here and willing to listen.

And she truly did need to vent.

So she talked. She explained that she and her ex-husband, Tate, had agreed that they both wanted kids and couldn't wait to start a family. "So we got married and bought a house. Time went by. Suddenly, it's five years after the wedding and I'm still on birth control."

He asked the logical question. "Why?"

"Tate said he wasn't ready. He traveled for work and he said his job was stressful. He needed time to get established before starting the family he said wanted so much. I kept after him. Finally, a year ago, he agreed to start trying. So we tried. A few months went by. I didn't get pregnant. We kept trying. But not all that hard. As I said, Tate traveled for work and he was gone a lot." And was Finn looking at her funny? She felt bold right then and wanted to be honest, so she just went ahead and asked him… "Are you thinking about the baby I lost when we were dating?"

His face flushed cherry red. "No! I didn't say that."

"But are you thinking about it?" She leaned in closer. "Finn, I can still have children. That was never the issue.

My doctor says there's no reason I won't conceive. Yes, I had a miscarriage back in high school." She'd lost the baby at the end of their senior year. And the experience had been heartbreaking—for her and for him, too. "But sometimes that happens in the early months of pregnancy. I promise you, there's no reason I can't have a successful pregnancy one of these days."

"Gotcha," he said. He looked really uncomfortable.

And now, she felt guilty. Just because she was feeling bold and honest didn't mean he had to be. "I'm oversharing, right?"

"Kenzie, no. You are not oversharing. Honestly."

"So…you're just dying to hear all this?"

He bobbed his head in a nod. "Yep. Go on."

"Okay, then." She shrugged. "It's pretty simple. Tate had begun making those not-ready-for-fatherhood noises again. And then, not all that long ago, out of the blue, Tate tells me that he's been doing some soul-searching and he's realized that marriage and kids aren't for him, after all. He asked for a divorce. And the next day, he moved out."

"Where is that jerk now?"

She gave a low laugh. "Remember. You asked."

"Yes, I did. Where is he?"

"As of now, Tate has moved back home to Denver after living in Vegas for six weeks to fulfill the residency requirement for our quickie divorce." She waved the papers at him again. "Which, as you can see, is now signed, sealed and delivered."

Finn proceeded to say all the right things—how Tate was a waste of space and somebody ought to make a quick trip to Denver to rearrange his face.

"I appreciate the support," she said mildly. "But the truth is, I'm glad that he's gone. It wasn't going to work. Yeah, it's a shock. I'll get over it, though. Today's a bad day but tomorrow will be better."

Finn was shaking his head. "If you say so..."

"I do."

"Fine, then. I'll hold myself back from paying your ex a little visit. But sheesh, no wonder you were feeling sick."

She realized she was actually glad that he'd followed her into the bar. "Honestly, Finn. Thanks for listening. I feel much better now." The ginger ale had really helped—as did having her high-school boyfriend's broad shoulder to cry on.

True, he'd walked away from her that summer right after high school. At the time, she'd nurtured a burning resentment toward him.

But not anymore. They honestly had been too young. Plus, he'd been as brokenhearted at the loss of their baby as she had. And his awful father, Finn Sr., hadn't helped the situation one bit. Finn's dad had big dreams for Finn and had constantly pressured him to move on, to leave Tenacity and his high-school girlfriend behind.

In hindsight, she could clearly see that Finn had done his best. He'd stepped up when she told him she was pregnant. He'd asked her to marry him, vowed that they would make it work somehow. He'd bought her a ring and they were both beginning to adjust to all the changes having the baby would bring—and then, four weeks later, the baby was gone.

It was an unexpected loss, one neither of them had known how to deal with. And now, years after all the pain and bitterness had passed, what stuck with her was the love. Because they *had* loved each other so much. More than they'd known how to deal with at the time.

Finn helped her on with her jacket and they left the Grizzly together.

Out on the street, a cool spring wind blew down from the north and the Montana sky was an endless wash of baby blue dotted here and there with fluffy white clouds. They paused on the sidewalk and faced each other.

"So," he said, "I have to tell you, for a woman who just got bad news in the mail, you are looking mighty fine."

"So nice of you to say so." She guided a loose curl of hair off her cheek and grinned up at him. In the bright, late-afternoon sunlight she could see that he still had that scar on the bridge of his nose from the time he'd gotten up close and personal with the face mask of a defensive lineman. The injury had occurred in a preseason scrimmage back in their junior year. She used to kiss that scar and whisper that it made him look super-hot and dangerous.

"It's good to see you," he said, those blue eyes holding hers.

"It's good to see you, too. Though I do owe you an apology."

"For what?"

"Are you kidding? I took shameless advantage of you. I made the last hour and a half all about me—along with a little detour into our sad, painful past."

"No apologies." He put on a stern look. "I asked you to tell me. I wanted to know how you've been."

"Well, then you definitely got what you asked for."

"Yes, I did." Oh, the way he was looking at her now.

Like there was no place he would rather be than standing on the sidewalk in front of the Grizzly with her.

She was vaguely aware of cars going by, people strolling along the sidewalk, too. Were they watching the reunion of the famous Finn Monahan and the girl he left behind?

So what if they were? Today had been a rough one. But then, Finn had followed her into the Grizzly and things had started looking up. She stepped a fraction closer, until there was less than an inch of daylight between them.

"I feel I should confess…" She let her voice trail off.

"Kenzie. Don't you dare stop there." His teasing threat made her laugh and his smile got wider.

She lifted her hands and rested them on his chest, felt the soft leather of his jacket and the strength of his body beneath it. "I watched every game when you were in the NFL—and I do mean starting with the very first one."

"I don't think I ever got on the field that first game."

She laughed again. "Still, it didn't take you long to be a star. Until the injury you were unstoppable…"

"Go ahead," he said in a growl. "Rub it in."

"Sorry, I didn't mean to bring up a tough subject. But I really did watch all your games, when you were in college and on through your years in the pros. I just… couldn't help myself—and I have no idea why I'm telling you all this." She started to step back.

Gently, he caught her arms. "Wait."

"What?"

"Damn, Kenzie. You're as beautiful as ever—scratch that. You are *more* beautiful than you were in high school.

And back then, there was no girl who could even hold a candle to you."

She could not resist. People were probably staring… but so what? She was a single woman again. And she could kiss whomever she pleased—even the big-shot jock who'd dumped her the summer after their senior year.

Kenzie lifted up on tiptoe. "Thank you…for listening."

And then, she kissed him.

It wasn't a deep kiss or even a long one, but it was oh, so very sweet. She breathed in the clean scent of his skin and reveled in the feel of his big arms around her.

Again. After all these years…

She dropped back onto her boot heels reluctantly. And he didn't let go. He still held her shoulders with those big, warm hands. His thumbs stroked lightly. She felt his touch acutely through the denim of her jacket.

He leaned close again. "Walk with me—where's your car?"

"Two blocks down, across the street."

"Let's go…"

They walked along in silence until they came parallel with her Bronco Sport, which she'd parked across the street. "My car's right there." They waited for an old pickup to rattle by and crossed together, stopping on the sidewalk next to her SUV.

He stuck his hands in his pockets and hunched his broad shoulders. Then he said almost shyly, "It's good to be home. It feels right. Like I'm coming full circle."

"I get it. I wouldn't live anywhere else—and I think somebody said you're selling real estate now?"

"That's right. I opened my own firm, Big Sky Properties. Are you looking for a house? If so, I'm your man."

"Sorry, but no. I love my house."

"Well, then. Let me know if you change your mind."

"Will do," she replied automatically and then gave him a slow, happy smile.

Because the way he was looking at her? It just...lit her up inside. For that moment, at least, the rumpled divorce decree she'd stuffed in her pocket didn't matter at all.

They both turned and leaned back against the Bronco with maybe a foot or so of distance between them. He moved a fraction closer.

The sleeve of his jacket brushed hers. And then he said softly, "How about dinner, you and me? For old times' sake..."

Suddenly, she felt downright audacious. And excited, too. She met his eyes directly. "Yes. I would like that."

"Excellent." He pulled out his phone and created a contact for her. When he passed it to her, she put in her number. And when she handed it back, he sent her a text.

Her phone chimed in her pocket. She pulled it out.

He'd written, I'll be seeing you. Soon.

She grinned. "Got it."

He tipped his hat and headed back up the street.

Kenzie drove home smiling, her earlier misery momentarily forgotten. No, she wasn't thinking of rekindling an old flame. But she liked this new, grown-up Finn. He'd been kind and attentive. He'd brightened her spirits on an otherwise deeply depressing day.

And really, the past was just that—over and done.

They could certainly share a nice dinner together. Maybe even become friends.

Yeah, he was more compelling than ever. No doubt he'd broken a long string of tender hearts in the years since they'd parted ways.

But so what? She wouldn't be falling for him again. Not a chance.

The minute Kenzie drove away, Finn started second-guessing his own actions.

He probably shouldn't have asked for her number. What had happened in the past still haunted him. And the ink was barely dry on her divorce.

No. Getting something going again with Kenzie would not be wise…

However, in the next several days he couldn't stop thinking about her. He grabbed his phone to reach out to her more than once…and then stuck the damn thing back in his pocket without following through.

Because she got to him. She always had. And now, he'd seen her again and he had to admit that he wanted to see her some more. He was just too damn interested in the girl he left behind and that was probably unwise.

He decided not to call. Instead, he worked a lot. Over the next week and a half, he closed three sales—a couple of ranchettes not too far from town and a bigger spread about fifty miles west of Tenacity. Business was booming. No doubt about it.

He also got a call from Barrett Deroy Jr. who had coached the local high-school football team last fall. Barrett talked him into getting together for a drink at the Tenacity Social Club.

When they got there, another town booster, Brent Woodson, was waiting for them.

The two men informed him that they wanted him to coach Tenacity High's varsity football team next season.

"I think this group of kids has real potential," Barrett said. "And with you stepping in as coach, big things can happen. You will give those boys the inspiration and training they need to make this season better than last year."

"Plus," added Brent, before Finn could gently say no, "you're in real estate, am I right?"

"Yes, I am. But I—"

"It matters that you're helping out in the community," said Barrett. "Your clients will love you for stepping up to coach the team."

"I really don't think so."

"But you will consider it, won't you?" asked Brent.

What could he say but, "Sure. Let me think about it…"

For a week, he tried *not* to think about it. Just like he tried not to think about Kenzie.

It didn't work. He thought about Kenzie a lot. And he thought about coaching the Titans, too.

Five days after Brent and Barrett took him out for that drink, he called Barrett and said yes.

Barrett laughed, "I knew you'd come through." They talked football for an hour, right there on the phone. Barrett agreed to be Finn's assistant coach.

It took him two more days to admit that he was acting like a total ass about Kenzie. He wanted to see her a lot—enough that it scared him. He'd been thinking that staying away would make thoughts of her fade. But that didn't happen. He wanted to see her again and the wanting was not going away.

He started to text her. But a text just seemed weak—

not to mention, nothing short of insulting. The least he could do was give her a chance to let his overdue call go to voicemail.

She picked up on the first ring. “Hello, Finn.”

Two words, *hello* and his name. From those two words, he knew everything. She sounded a million miles away and she was not glad to hear from him.

He considered faking it, making small talk, playing it light and easy. But they had loved each other once, even if they were barely more than kids at the time. She deserved honesty from him.

“I know I should have called sooner,” he said. “I wanted to call. Maybe too much. Truth is, it kind of freaks me out, how much I want to see you again.”

“It’s okay, Finn.” Her voice was kind now. But it was distant, too. “You did nothing wrong.”

He couldn’t read her. And this was not going as he’d hoped. He had to do something, so he went for it. “Are you free tomorrow night? Or Friday night? I could do Thursday, too. We could—”

“Finn,” she said, cutting him off. “Listen. It was good to see you that day at the Grizzly. But since then, I’ve had to take a long, hard look at…things.”

No doubt about it. This was going nowhere good. “What things?”

“Well, I have to be realistic. I just got divorced. I can’t be getting anything started right now. I really can’t.”

“And that’s fine.” It wasn’t fine. Not in the least. But he understood why she was turning him down. They had a painful history together. That in itself would make a woman wary. And now he’d waffled like a fool and taken too long to call her after implying that he would be getting right back in touch. He didn't blame her for not wanting to start in with him again. Still, he gave it one more shot. "I mean, we can be friends, right?"

She sighed then. "Oh, Finn. I don't think so."

What could he say? "Well. Alright, then." It wasn't alright. But he did understand. He'd blown it, pure and simple.

"It's just…" Her voice trailed off.

"Just what, Kenzie?" He kept his tone gentle.

"It's a bad idea for us to get all buddy-buddy. And not because of what happened fifteen years ago."

"Tell the truth," he coaxed. "You're pissed because I'm a jerk who took way too damn long to call."

"No. Honestly, I'm not pissed at you, not at all."

"So then, have dinner with me."

Several painful seconds crawled by. Finally, she said, "I'm not ready to go out with any guy, not even for old times' sake. Not even as friends. I need to…focus on myself right now. My life is changing and I can't afford unnecessary complications."

So now, he was both unnecessary *and* a complication? He really had blown it. He'd felt such a connection with her that day at the Grizzly.

But now what could he say? "Right. I'll let you go then."

"Finn, honestly, I—"

"Kenzie. It's okay. You said no. And I get it."

Dead silence on her end. And then, she said, "Of course. I understand. Take care of yourself."

"You too," he replied.

And that was it. She disconnected the call.

* * *

But Tenacity was a small town. He was bound to run into her now and then.

On a rainy day toward the end of May, he saw her at Tenacity Grocery. He glanced up from tossing a box of Raisin Bran into his cart and there she was coming his way.

He thought how pretty she looked in jeans, a white shirt and a hooded canvas jacket, with her long blond hair pulled back in a low ponytail. At the last minute, as the distance between their carts shrank to a couple of feet, he remembered to put on a smile.

She said, “Hello, Finn.”

“Kenzie.” He gave her a nod and kept moving forward.

The building was an old one, the aisles narrow enough that the wheels of their carts almost touched. He got a faint hint of her perfume—vanilla and oranges—and took special care not to look back at her once she had rolled on by.

A few weeks later, he spotted her having lunch with three other women in the Silver Spur Café. He’d come in to pick up a take-out order and saw her there by the window that looked out on Central Avenue. She was laughing at something Lauren Dalton, who taught science at the high school, had said.

He couldn’t stop himself from staring. As Kenzie threw back her head, her pale hair gleamed in the sunlight that streamed through the window behind her. Her happy laughter captivated him. He made himself turn away so that she wouldn’t catch him watching her. As luck would have it, his take-out order was right there waiting for him. He grabbed it and got the hell out of there.

Then, in the first week of August, he came face-to-face with her at the high school, which he'd figured would happen eventually. They met up at the entrance that led directly into the administrative wing. He was going in and she was on her way out.

"Kenzie." He tipped his hat as he held the door open for her to go through.

"Thank you, Finn."

"You're welcome."

By then, she was already walking away. He just stood there holding the door wide open, staring at her retreating back as she strode purposefully along the front walkway, heading for the parking lot. The sun made her hair into a waterfall of gold down her back. She wore a filmy, light-as-air shirt with fluttery sleeves and a full skirt that fell to mid-calf. Her boots were tooled with flowers. He watched her go and wished…

What the hell did it matter what he wished? She'd shut him down and he didn't blame her for it. There was nothing to wish for.

And he really needed to remember that.

Chapter One

The present, mid-August

First day of preseason football practice dawned clear and warm. The weather forecast looked good with variable winds and a high around eighty degrees. By 7:30 a.m., Finn had the entire varsity squad out on the field.

He started with an introductory pep talk. It went pretty well, he thought. The kids were eager and engaged. No horsing around, no attitude, everybody ready to listen and learn.

He was just about to move on to warm-ups when he glanced toward the stands and spotted Kenzie on the sidelines talking to the water boy. For a moment, he wondered if he'd maybe lost his mind.

But no. It was Kenzie. She was really there. She had that blond hair pinned back in a neat bun, and she wore blue scrub pants and an oversize scrub top printed with footballs. A wheeled black medical bag waited at her side.

About then, he put it together. The team had no doctor or training staff. Kenzie had stepped up to handle first aid on the field.

The water boy, whose name was Oscar Abernathy, said something to her. She grinned wide and nodded.

Just then, a gust of wind tried to free her hair from that tidy little bun and plastered the football-printed scrub top to her body.

"Okay," Finn said, still looking where he shouldn't be. "A few stretches and then we'll..." Words deserted him as he noticed that Kenzie had put on a few pounds—mostly around the middle. The sight of that newly rounded belly of hers told him everything. "It's important to..." His voice trailed off again as he noted that her breasts were fuller, too.

Barrett Deroy Jr. stood several yards away. Finn signaled him close.

Barrett jogged over. "What do you need, Coach?"

"Take over for a minute or two, would you? Get them going on the warm-ups?"

"You got it." Barrett faced the squad. "Okay, guys. Spread out. We'll start nice and easy with marching in place..."

Finn didn't hear what Barrett said next. By then, he'd tuned everything out but the school nurse in her football-themed scrub top as he jogged to the sidelines, where Kenzie was still chatting with Oscar.

Their eyes met. "Nurse Osborne, I need a minute."

She gave him a cordial smile. If he hadn't been hopelessly in love with her once, he would have had no clue that smile was forced. "Of course, Coach."

He turned to the water boy. "Hey, Oscar."

"Hi, Coach!"

"I'm through giving speeches. You ready to keep the team hydrated?"

"I'm on it, Coach." Oscar grabbed his water carrier

full of squeeze bottles from the first row of the bleachers and jogged onto the field.

Now, it was just Finn and Kenzie—and he needed to say something casual and innocuous. *So how are you doing?* Or maybe, *'Preciate you helping out like this.*

But the way she was looking at him said she knew exactly what he was really thinking and there was no point in pretending he didn't.

So he just put it right out there. "How pregnant are you?"

She answered with a weary shrug. "Twenty-four weeks tomorrow." They stared at each other. After several awkward seconds, she added, "And, no, Finn. That day at the Grizzly, I had no idea I was having my ex's baby. I didn't even think about it as a possibility until a few days later. So I took a test and saw my doctor. By the time you called, everything had changed for me."

"I get it." He studied her beautiful face. "And I wasn't asking you to explain all that."

She lifted her chin in defiance. "But you wanted to know."

He gave her the truth. "Yeah. I did. How are you feeling? Are you and the baby alright?"

She looked so proud, standing there with her head high and the wind tugging at her pinned-back hair. He ached to comfort her somehow, though it was obvious she had no desire to take comfort from him right now.

The past—*their* past—felt so close at the moment, pressing in on them. He asked again, "Are you okay?"

"Please. I'm pregnant, not ill." She dared a step closer and lowered her voice even more. "This isn't then. I'm fine, Finn. I really am." She rested her hand on her belly.

"I've had two ultrasounds. It's a girl and she's doing great."

His eyes teared up. Must be the wind. "Yeah?"

"Yeah. And I'm happy," she whispered. "I want a family. And now, I'm going to have one."

"Well, then. That's good. Real good…" He tried to think of something thoughtful and understanding to say. Finally, he offered, "If you need anything, if there's anything I can do, you give me a call."

She looked at him levelly. "I meant what I just said. I am okay, honestly. But thank you for offering."

"Your husband…?"

"*Ex*-husband," she corrected him. "And nothing's changed on that front."

He should keep his damn mouth shut. But he asked, anyway. "Does he know?"

She nodded. "I called him. He said the same thing he said when he asked for a divorce. He doesn't want marriage and he definitely doesn't want children." She swiped a windblown lock of hair away from her soft lips. "Tate is totally out of the picture."

"Good, then. Great…" He almost groaned at his own words. *Great?* Her ex-husband had decided to walk away from her and their baby. And he called it *great*?

Tipping her head toward the field, where Barrett had the team doing arm circles, she suggested, "They're waiting on you."

"I have to ask…"

She sighed. "Of course, you do. What?"

"Did you know you were pregnant when I finally called you last spring?"

"I did, yes."

"And is the baby the real reason you turned me down that day?"

She made a thoughtful little sound. "Yeah—but it didn't help that you took so long to call."

He winced. "Got it." He shook his head. "I had no idea you would be helping out on the field."

"I love football." She actually smiled.

"I remember." He said the words quietly. They stared at each other, the past a living thing between them. Their junior and senior years, she'd been head cheerleader and she'd never missed a game.

"I try to pitch in where I'm needed," she added.

"Well, and that's great. That you're here to help out. Thank you, I mean that. And I'm really glad that things are going well for you…" He kind of ran out of words. "Well." He coughed to clear the sudden lump in his throat. "I'd better get back to the team." At her slow nod, he turned and jogged away.

Through the rest of that first practice, Finn's thoughts strayed more than once to the bleachers where Kenzie sat with her medical bag at her feet. He kept wondering, how was she, really? She said she was happy to be having a child. And he believed her.

But still, it couldn't be easy being on her own. Having a baby should be a team effort, shouldn't it? Helping a child go from diapers to adulthood was a big job. A woman needed a real partner for that.

But then he thought of his own mom and dad, who, along with his younger brothers, Eric and Dan, had relocated to Florida years ago. His mother was a good woman. She was always there anytime her boys needed her.

His dad, though? Finn Monahan Sr. saw the world as

purely transactional. He "loved" the people who made his life better, the people who served him, the people he could use to get ahead…and the people who made him look good.

When Finn had been an up-and-coming football star, Finn Sr. was always checking in. But when Finn left the game behind and started selling real estate, his father had stopped calling.

Finn's mom kept in touch, though. And when she did, she inevitably made excuses for his dad.

But Finn knew the score. Finn Sr. was an important man with a busy schedule. He'd never been the kind of father who had a lot of time for his sons. Essentially, his mom had raised her boys alone, same as Kenzie said she planned to do.

Again, he found himself hoping that she really was okay with being a single parent. True, women raised their kids on their own all the time. But it really did seem like a lot for a woman with a full-time job to take on.

No doubt her friends would step up when needed, and her folks were good people. He was sure they'd be there to help when the baby was born.

Hell. *He* would help if she'd only let him…

That thought gave him pause.

Because as it turned out, they were going to be seeing a lot of each other right here on the football field all through the season. And maybe, over time, she might reconsider the idea of the two of them becoming friends.

Yeah, she'd made it painfully clear that they would never be a couple again. But hey. If he played his cards right she just might end up deciding that she could always use a friend.

* * *

That night was the beginning of team-bonding weekend. The squad and the coaching staff slept right there at the high school. Community boosters provided meals and cots. The players and staff brought their own sleeping bags. Only Kenzie went home for the night.

But she was back first thing Saturday morning to have breakfast with the rest of them. Finn admired her team spirit. And he couldn't stop thinking about her, wondering how she was doing, hoping she really was feeling fine about having her baby on her own.

More than once, he found himself staring at her, hoping that despite everything, they might end up being friends. And kind of wanting to kick his own ass for messing up and waiting so long to reach out to her last spring.

And Kenzie wasn't the only one Finn couldn't stop wondering about. He also wanted to know more about Oscar Abernathy. The kid was laser-focused on his job, always ready with a water bottle whenever a player, Barrett or Finn signaled the need for one.

Oscar also seemed to know a lot about football. The boy was a fountain of football stats, which he frequently offered under his breath to no one in particular. And he seemed very…self-contained, even a bit withdrawn somehow, kind of off in his own world. He had no close friends—at least not any of the players on the team. Finn wanted to know more about him and kept meaning to quiz Barrett, but the opportunity to discuss the water boy never presented itself.

Saturday was packed with activities. Finn had no time to focus on anything but getting a head start on crafting a program that would coax the most out of every member of the team.

Late that afternoon, he praised his players before sending them off to rest and recuperate, so they would be fresh on Monday, when the work would begin all over again. After everyone had left the field, he headed home, aka the Rawlings place. It was seven miles outside of town. On twenty rolling acres, the property included a red barn, an empty horse pasture and a sparsely furnished four-thousand-square-foot house full of big rooms he never entered.

But hey. He'd been an NFL superstar once with more than one big-ass house. Since then, it was kind of a habit with him to live in a house with way more room than he was ever going to need.

That night, Finn ate leftovers and stayed up late working on his plans for future practices, then caught up on paperwork for his real-estate business.

Sunday he hit the ground running, showing houses with acreage to two clients and submitting two offers. He couldn't help thinking that between coaching the Titans and his job selling real estate, he barely had time to eat and sleep.

But finally, Sunday evening, he got a few precious hours to himself—in his too-large, too-empty house. After a take-out dinner of *pollo asado* from the great little Mexican restaurant in town, he did what he'd been working up the nerve to do for months now.

He called Kenzie—because, he reassured himself, he wanted to find out a little bit more about Oscar. Yeah, he could have called Barrett, but by the time he reminded himself that Barrett was the one he'd been planning to ask, he'd already hit the call button for Kenzie.

She picked up on the second ring. "Finn."

"It's clear from the way you just said my name that you're not glad to hear from me." He was grinning.

She knew it, too. "Wipe that smirk off your face."

"Sheesh, Kenz. Fifteen years have gone by since we were together. And still, you don't have to see my face to know that I'm smirking."

"What do you want?"

"I love it when a woman can't wait to get rid of me."

"Oh, come on. I didn't say that."

"But you were thinking it."

She scoffed. "So you're calling to give me grief, is that it?"

"Nope."

"Then what?"

"Well, first off, I want to apologize. I was abrupt at first practice the other day...about the, uh, baby, I mean. Until I spotted you on the field I had no idea you were pregnant, that you must have been pregnant that day we met up at the Grizzly."

"That day at the Grizzly, I didn't know that I was pregnant, either. I didn't even consider that I might be pregnant until a couple of days later. That was when finally I went out and bought a few tests. And when the stick turned blue I still didn't believe it. I took a second test just to be sure." Her voice was softer now. "I should have been honest that day you called me. I should have told you the truth, that I'd just learned I was pregnant, that everything had changed for me. However, in my defense..." There was a long silence.

Had she hung up? "Kenzie?"

"Right here—and it just occurred to me that I sound completely self-absorbed."

"No, you don't."

"It's nice of you to say that, but still. You don't need to know every little thing I'm going through."

"Maybe not," he said. "But I *want* to know about it—if that counts at all."

"Oh, Finn..."

"Come on. Lay it on me."

"Are you serious?"

"Yes." He was grinning again now. "Talk to me, Kenzie."

"Alright. But remember, you asked."

"I did ask. And I'm listening."

"Well, the truth is, I'd only gotten the test results from my doctor the day before you called. And then, I'd talked to my ex. That wasn't fun. Truthfully, that day you called, I was still kind of reeling from all of it, if you know what I mean..."

"Yeah. I can understand that." He resisted the urge to say bad things about her ex and instead added mildly, "I appreciate your filling me in."

"Sure—so we're good, then?"

"We are. We're solid."

"I'm glad." She sounded pleased, which made him feel better about everything.

"Me, too," he said. "And I have a question..."

"Sure. Fire away."

"I've been wondering about Oscar Abernathy..."

Kenzie stared at the flat screen mounted over her fireplace. Before taking Finn's call, she'd muted the sound.

Now, she pointed the remote again and the screen went black. "Oscar? What about him?"

"Well, for one thing, I think that kid might know more about football than I do."

"Not possible!" She was faking extreme shock for all she was worth. "Nobody knows more about football than the great Finn Monahan!"

"Yeah, well. I couldn't believe it, either…at first. But I swear, that kid has a firm grasp of DVOA."

"DV-what?"

"Defense-adjusted value over average."

"Well, that really clears things up for me…not." She laughed and then added more seriously, "Okay, I've heard of it. But you should explain it to me, anyway."

"Fair enough. It's essentially a system that puts statistics in context. DVOA can predict outcomes more consistently than simple stats like total touchdowns or rushing yards."

"And you're saying that Oscar understands this system?"

"Yeah. I believe he does."

That surprised her—not that Oscar understood some complex statistical system. But that Finn had taken an interest in Oscar Abernathy. Back in high school, Finn never would have spared a second thought for Oscar—and no, Finn hadn't been a mean boy. He'd always treated others kindly, with respect. But he'd also been far too wrapped up in his own plans and goals to show much interest in the team water boy.

"Kenzie? You still with me?"

She smiled to herself. "I am right here."

"So, then. Will you tell me about Oscar?"

"Sure. He's smart and conscientious, a good guy, observant and kind. His mom died about a decade ago. And he and his dad, Jesse, moved to town recently. You should also be aware that Oscar is autistic, though he's considered low-support."

Finn responded cautiously. "Okay…"

"I've met with both Oscar and his dad to talk about Oscar's individual health-care needs."

"This is sounding very official."

She laughed but then said seriously, "Because it is. I'm only telling you this because you're on staff at the high school and Oscar's welfare is your professional concern. Basically, he might get a bit more overstimulated than other kids, and we've established supports for him like the use of headphones and earplugs for loud noises."

"Got it. And thanks for filling me in."

"No problem. Honestly, Finn. Oscar gets along well enough with everyone to avoid much attention, so a lot of people in town overlook him. Plus, as I already said, he's new here. He does seem to be doing pretty well, but as of yet he doesn't have a lot of friends. I guess what I'm saying is that Oscar doesn't have a built-in support network here, and he could use someone who appreciates his passions, one of which is football."

"We have that in common, Oscar and me!"

She smiled at that. "Yes, though I think you'll find Oscar knows even more than you do."

"Alright. I look forward to being continually humbled by Oscar's superior knowledge of the game."

Dear God in heaven, Finn Monahan could be charming when he wanted to be.

She drew a slow, careful breath and said brightly, "Happy to help."

"And Kenzie..."

"Hmm?"

"Well, how are you doing—I mean, what with having a baby and all? Are you feeling good, eating right?"

"Oh, Finn. Thanks for asking. Honestly, I am doing great and so is the baby."

"Well, then. That's terrific. And now I know that you're feeling good, there's just one more thing I need to ask before I let you go."

"I'm listening."

"Won't you please have dinner with me?"

She pressed her lips together in order to keep the word *yes* from escaping.

He let her silence go on for several painful seconds, then coaxed, "Come on. It's just dinner. How about Tuesday night? We'll go to that new steak house."

She really did mean to say *no*. And yet somehow, when she opened her mouth, *yes* made a break for it.

"That's what I wanted to hear." He sounded so pleased. She could just picture him right now, a cocky smirk on his face, those blue eyes gleaming.

And all of a sudden, she was thrown back in time to their first real date, freshman year. They were both just fifteen and he didn't have his driver's license yet. Luckily, the house he grew up in had been only five blocks from hers, and hers happened to be right around the corner from the Silver Spur Café.

When she'd answered the door, he was standing on the welcome mat, his hair slicked back with way too much styling gel. In his right fist, he held a wilted bouquet of wild blanket flowers.

Even slightly droopy, those daisy-like flowers were beautiful, the bright orange petals tipped in sunny yellow. He'd handed them over. "For you, Kenzie."

When she took them from him, the stems were damp from his sweaty palms. She knew then that Finn Monahan *liked* her. And that was a wonderful thing. Because she liked him right back.

"I'll pick you up at six." His voice—a man's voice now—jerked her back to the present.

She blinked away the tender memory and announced, "My treat."

"Nice try, Kenz," he replied dryly. "And no way. I did the asking, I get the check. Tuesday night. I'll be knocking on your door at six."

She debated insisting that she would meet him there… but why? If he wanted to pick her up *and* buy her dinner, so be it. She rattled off her address.

"Great. Got it," he said. "See you at practice." And then he was gone.

On Monday, Finn pushed his players hard…but not too hard. He wanted to get them in condition, not injure or overstress them. At the end of practice, though, he and Barrett put on the pressure. It never hurt to test a player's limits in a carefully managed, responsible way.

That day, Oscar was every bit as conscientious about keeping the team hydrated as he'd been the week before. Finn created a couple of chances to chat with him briefly—or maybe *chat* was the wrong word. Oscar was not the least bit chatty. He said what he meant and he moved on.

"Coach, I'm working on my own app to organize the team's stats," Oscar announced when Finn asked him how he was doing. "There are some good basic apps out there for high-school teams, yeah. But they're by subscription and the free ones are always getting shut down."

Finn waited a beat to be certain Oscar had stopped talking, because it seemed to him that the boy tensed up a bit when interrupted. "Everybody on staff will get the GameChanger app for free this year," Finn said. GameChanger was currently the most popular recording, scheduling and communication app for high-school football teams. "And you are officially on staff."

Oscar frowned. And then, he nodded. "That's great, Coach. But I want to design my own app, too."

"Alrighty, then. Go for it."

Oscar regarded him solemnly. "Thanks, Coach. I will." And off he went to fill bottles.

Finn didn't get a chance that day to check in with Kenzie. She was right there, though, on the sidelines, ready to wrap a minor sprain and bandage a cut when needed. Twice, he managed to catch her eye. Both times, he grinned at her. She stared back at him with a straight facc. That only made him grin wider. He couldn't wait for tomorrow night and their friends-only dinner out.

After practice, he and Barrett met briefly to discuss training strategies. Then Finn had some things to take care of at Big Sky Properties. He spent a few hours there.

He got back to his place around five. One of these days, he thought as he walked in and stared at the mostly empty living area, he needed to buy a new sofa and some good leather chairs. What furniture he had now consisted mostly of things the former owners had left behind.

The only room he'd put any effort into was the primary bedroom. It looked pretty good, he thought. But he couldn't hang out in there all the time.

His phone rang as he was sticking leftover takeout in the microwave. He shut the microwave door and took the phone from his pocket.

Great. Just what he needed on a solitary Monday evening in his empty house. A rare, completely unexpected and most likely unpleasant call from his dad.

"Hi, Dad. How are you doing?"

"I'm doing well, son. Always." His dad was a banker. Years before, Finn Monahan Sr. had run the Tenacity branch of Big Western Bank. Then, not long after Finn headed off to the University of Michigan, his dad had moved the rest of the family to Florida, where he'd taken the reins of a bigger bank. Finn Sr. had been moving up the banking food chain ever since. Now, he was president of the largest bank and trust in Tampa. "Tell me, son. How's the real-estate business going?"

Finn suppressed a weary sigh. He knew the question was a setup. Still, why be negative? He answered as though his father really cared. "Thanks, I'm doing well. Things are really picking up around here."

"I'm sure." His dad sounded bored to death.

Finn bragged on his town anyway. "There's the new Dinosaur Center and there's also been a discovery of kimberlite, a source of unmined diamonds. Tenacity is coming back from hard times. And my business is booming."

"Booming is a relative term, wouldn't you say?" his dad asked.

"Depends on how you look at it," Finn answered pleasantly. "What can I do for you, Dad?"

"Just be honest with me, son."

"Of course."

"Are you staging a comeback?" All of a sudden, Finn Sr. actually sounded eager.

The question was so unexpected, Finn scoffed. "A comeback from what?"

"Tell the truth, now. I saw your interview in *The Lewistown News-Argus.*"

Finn remembered then. A reporter from the Lewistown paper had interviewed him a couple of weeks ago for a short piece about his decision to coach the Titans this season. "Back up a minute. Are you telling me that you subscribe to the Lewistown paper?"

"Of course not," his dad replied dismissively. "But I do occasionally surf the internet. I like to know what my boys are up to."

"You know, you could just call me and ask me what I'm up to, Dad. I would be happy to answer any and all questions you might have about my life."

Finn Sr. ignored that suggestion and muttered, "You were the best. You should have been a legend. *Time* magazine called you a phenom. Until your injury, you could do no wrong. But you gave up and now, you're selling houses."

"And you're a banker, Dad. It's called making a living. We all have to pay the rent somehow."

"Don't take that attitude with me."

Finn drew a slow, careful breath. "How about this, Dad? Tell me how *you've* been."

A long silence, then he replied, "Your mother and I are fine."

"Good. I'm glad to hear it. Give her my love."

"I will…and the other line is ringing. I need to get that."

"Okay, Dad." He should say "good talking to you." But he couldn't quite bring himself to tell that lie. "Take care."

"Right." And that was it. His father ended the call.

As for Finn, he poured himself two fingers of very good Scotch and sat in one of his left-behind living-room chairs. As he stared out the big picture window at the rustic rail fence that surrounded the house and the rolling pastureland beyond it, he sipped his drink slowly and thought that he really did like being back home in Tenacity.

He enjoyed helping people and he liked selling real estate. And football season hadn't even begun yet, but he was already having a ball coaching the home team.

Plus, tomorrow night, he was going out to dinner with Kenzie—no, it wasn't a date. And that was okay. They might actually become good friends.

Hey. Stranger things had happened.

As for his father, never again would Finn let himself feel hurt that his dad rarely called anymore. In fact, it would be alright with Finn if his father never called again.

Chapter Two

Finn had a closing on Tuesday morning. So on Monday after practice, he'd asked Barrett to take over until Finn got there, hopefully around ten.

"Absolutely," Barrett had said. "I'll keep things moving along."

The closing was finished on time and Finn headed straight for the high school. When he arrived on the field, the first thing he looked for was his favorite nurse.

But Kenzie wasn't there. A burly guy in a tactical shirt with a Tenacity Fire and Rescue patch on the sleeve stood on the sidelines instead. He carried an orange first-responder bag and looked more than ready to step in if called upon to provide first aid.

That the team had medical help on the sidelines was all Finn really needed to know. For one reason or another, Kenzie couldn't be there. As long as she'd found someone to sub in for her, no big deal.

Or it shouldn't be.

But it was, damn it.

Because, well, what if something bad had happened? What if she was really sick? What if there had been some issue with the baby?

She lived alone. Yeah, she had a lot of friends in town,

and that eased his mind a little. If she needed help for some reason, she would no doubt have a list of people she could call.

But still. He couldn't stand the idea that she might be sick or hurt. That the baby might…

He refused to complete that thought. Because he knew he was overreacting. This wasn't the summer after their senior year. She was fine and the baby was fine.

But just to be sure, he left Barrett to work with the team for another few minutes and introduced himself to the bearded EMT, whose name was Rufus. As they shook hands, Finn asked, "So where's Kenzie? Is she okay?"

"Yeah, far as I know. Something about a routine doctor's appointment…"

Routine. That was good, right?

Of course, it was. If she was sick or if something had gone wrong with the baby, she would have called him, wouldn't she? At least she would have let him know that she had to cancel their dinner date.

Which wasn't a date. Uh-uh. Just two friends sharing a companionable meal. Nothing to see here…

"You sure she's alright?" he asked Rufus again.

"Honestly, man. She seemed fine. You know what *I* know."

"Okay, then. I appreciate your filling in for her."

"Hey, no problem. Happy to help. My boy's on the team—Darren Tuttle?"

"Darren. Of course." Finn took a minute to talk to Rufus about his son. Darren was a big, strong kid, who had shown up for tryouts, unsure of which position to go for. Finn had explained that Darren didn't have to name his preferred position immediately. They wouldn't be choosing the starting lineup until much closer to the first game of the season.

The truth was, Finn already had Darren pegged as a linebacker. But that choice could change due to any number of factors.

"We're all excited to have you in charge of the team this year, Coach," said Rufus.

"I'm honored to hear that," Finn replied. He and Rufus shook hands and then Finn jogged over to join the team on the field, where Barrett had set up an endurance circuit.

The players worked through the circuit as Barrett shouted instructions and encouragement. As for Finn, he just stood there, staring at nothing, worrying about Kenzie.

Rufus had said she was fine. The guy was an EMT. If there was some problem, Rufus would have picked up on it. Hell, Kenzie would have told Rufus that she wasn't feeling well.

Wouldn't she?

Of course, she would. There was nothing to get all worked up about. But Finn got worked up, anyway.

He kept telling himself he was being an idiot and nothing bad was happening to Kenzie or her baby. It didn't help. He kept stewing. The apprehension made him sick to his stomach. The past was crowding him, taunting him. He would never forget how it had been, that she'd felt under the weather for a couple of days—she'd felt achy, she'd said. And she was cramping. She'd been unable to sleep at night.

And then, she'd started bleeding and…

He hadn't realized how much he'd wanted their baby

until the baby was gone. After that, he just wanted to get away, to forget what they'd lost. But he'd never forgotten, not really. That loss was part of him and always would be.

Barrett stepped close. "You okay?"

"All good—but I need to make a quick call."

Barrett peered at him more closely. "What is it, Finn? What's wrong?"

"I just...have to check on something." He needed to know for sure that nothing bad had happened to Kenzie or the baby.

"Alright..." Barrett had a funny look on his face, probably because Finn's anxiety was way too plain to see.

"Long story," said Finn through clenched teeth. "Just...don't ask. Please?"

"Got it," said Barrett. "No problem. Make your call."

Finn pulled his phone from his pocket and headed for the sidelines just as Kenzie, in dark blue scrubs with her hair pulled back in the usual tidy bun, breezed through the north gate onto the field. She was pulling her black wheeled bag and she looked perfectly healthy.

Sheepishly, his heartbeat roaring in his ears, Finn slipped his phone back into his pocket.

Kenzie went straight to Rufus. When she reached him, they shared a few words. The EMT was on his way to the gate before Finn's racing heart finally slowed to an easier rhythm.

Kenzie spotted him then. She gave him a wave and a dazzling smile. He waved right back as Barrett asked, "All good?"

"Yeah," Finn replied with a long, slow breath. He wanted to jog right over there, but he held himself back. It was obvious that Kenzie's routine doctor's appointment had been just that. She didn't need him falling all over her no matter how much he longed for absolute proof that she and the baby were doing fine. "Everything's great," he said. And it was. Now wasn't then. Kenzie's baby was safe and so was she.

He tipped his head toward the hardworking players as they pushed through a sprint and then dropped to the ground for burpees. "Think they're ready for a break?"

"Couldn't hurt," Barrett said with a nod. "I've worked them pretty hard."

"Okay, let's take a huddle and talk aims and objectives..."

Kenzie's house, on the east side of town, had a cute picket fence around a tidy patch of lawn and a cozy front porch complete with a porch swing. The welcome mat was printed with bright flowers.

Kenzie opened the door before he had a chance to knock. "Right on time." She stepped back. "Come in, come in..."

"This is nice," Finn said as she closed the door behind him.

He took in the open living area. There was a stone fireplace, oak floors and gorgeous wool area rugs woven with decorative vines and geometric shapes. The sofa and chairs faced the fireplace. Through the arch at the back of the room, he could see a dining area with a Craftsman-style table. Beyond that there was an island that marked off the business end of the kitchen.

"Homey," he said. "And I mean that in the best way."

"I like it here." She glanced around, grinning. "And since Tate couldn't wait to get out of town, he had zero problem agreeing that I should get the house. Come on. I'll give you the ten-cent tour."

He followed her into the kitchen, which was as cozy as the living area, with two windows on the sidewall looking out on the thick trunk and leafy branches of a mature oak tree. She had an office space on the main floor.

The primary bedroom was there, too. It was nice and roomy, that bedroom. She had a king-size bed with nightstands on both sides. There was a rocking chair by the window, a walk-in closet and a good-size attached bath.

From there, she led him upstairs, where there were two more small bedrooms, another bathroom and a loft area.

"It's a great house," he said when they'd reached the main floor again.

"We were lucky to get it." She frowned. He wondered if she was thinking of her ex-husband, of the life they had shared in this charming bungalow. But then she grinned. "And now, it's all mine." She hesitated a moment before she said, "I guess we should probably head for the restaurant, huh?"

Was she nervous? Because all of a sudden, he sure was. Absurdly so. He allowed himself one last glance around her cozy, inviting living room and gestured her ahead of him. "After you."

As they went down the front walk to Finn's waiting pickup, Kenzie suggested, "It's nice out and it's only a few blocks to the restaurant. Why don't we just walk over there."

"Great idea." He dared to tuck her hand in the crook of his elbow…and felt like a million bucks when she wrapped her fingers around his arm.

Satterfield's Steak House, on Central Avenue not far from the Grizzly, had a heavy wooden front door painted a lustrous black with leaded glass lights on either side. Inside, booths lined one wall of the dining room. On the other there were tables covered with snow-white linen tablecloths. A small bar ran half the length of the back wall and copper pendant lights gave the place a warm, inviting glow.

"I like this," Kenzie said as the hostess led them to one of the two unoccupied booths.

The woman—the owner, as it turned out—introduced herself as Ruby Satterfield. "Just call me Ruby." She was slim and tall with lustrous black hair and dark brown skin, and she might have been anywhere from thirty-five to fifty. "We're new here and we're so glad to be a part of this community," she said.

"Your restaurant is beautiful," Kenzie replied.

"Thank you—best steaks in the Treasure State," Ruby said. "I've put my name on the place, so you know I'm not kidding."

Finn was nodding. "You've made a big hit in town. Everyone says the food here is excellent."

"That's what we like to hear." Beaming, Ruby handed them menus, rattled off a couple of specials and assured them that their server would be right with them.

Once she was gone, Kenzie leaned toward him. "Things are definitely looking up in Tenacity."

"It's about time."

The steaks were juicy and tender. As for the house salad drizzled with vinaigrette dressing and the twice-baked potatoes? Equally delicious.

Finn enjoyed the meal. However, he couldn't help worrying a little about Kenzie. She'd seemed fine after her visit to the doctor and he'd promised himself he wouldn't hover. But was she really okay?

When their server cleared the plates away, Finn ordered a second whiskey and Kenzie said yes to a decaf with cream.

The waitress left and Kenzie asked quietly, "Is something wrong?"

He started to lie and say there was nothing. But he looked in her shining eyes and somehow the truth slipped out. "I was surprised to see Rufus on the sidelines in your place this morning. He said you had a routine doctor's appointment. And I did kind of wonder if you were… alright?"

She blinked and leaned closer. "Finn. I'm fine. Honestly. And Rufus is great. If one of the players gets injured he will know what to do."

"I believe you." Finn sipped his drink. "I'm sure Rufus is perfectly competent."

"So, then, what were you worried about?"

"I just thought maybe you had some issue—you know, with the baby. That maybe you weren't, uh, feeling well."

Her blue eyes got misty. "Oh, Finn…" She reached out.

He grabbed her hand like a lifeline. "You're okay, then? There's no problem?"

"Finn. What happened fifteen years ago is not going to happen again."

He shut his mouth to keep from asking how she could be sure of that.

But damned if she didn't read his mind, anyway. "I don't have any kind of chronic issue. And I'm well past fourteen weeks, by which time eighty percent of miscarriages happen."

"Right," he said. And the past was there, in the space between them, as fresh and painful as an open wound. They'd lost their baby at fourteen weeks.

That loss had been the end of them—of their love that was supposed to last forever. Of the life they'd planned together. Of all the promises they'd made to each other.

His father had really gone after him then. Finn Sr. had urged him to let the past go and reach for the future. And Finn had wanted to go, wanted to leave all the pain and heartache behind. Three weeks after their baby was no more, he broke up with her and headed off to college in Michigan. He'd always been sure she must have hated him for that.

But right now, those eyes of hers only spoke of sadness and understanding. "I mean it," she said. "Believe me. All the tests show that this baby is doing great, growing normally. Today was a regular checkup—one that's been scheduled for weeks."

He asked, "So…you're feeling good then?"

She made a joke of it. "What I'm feeling is enormous. And please stop looking at me like I might need an ambulance any minute now. I am fine. My baby is fine."

The tension in his shoulders eased and he allowed himself a slow, deep breath. "Okay, then. That's great." He even managed a smile as he picked up his drink. "Here's to… What's her name, anyway?"

"I haven't decided yet. I mean, I keep making a choice…and then changing my mind."

"Well, alright then. Here's to your little girl."

She raised her coffee cup and tapped it gently to his glass. "To my little girl." They both drank.

And then, for several seconds they just sat there, looking at each other across the white tablecloth. He felt the echo of the past acutely. Of all the things he hadn't said, the choices he'd made then that he might have made differently.

Yeah, he'd followed his big dream, even had some success at it. But right now, with his gaze locked on hers, all he could think of was how much he had loved her, how he'd let ambition and grief and the relentless power of his father's will make his choice for him. How different would things be now if he'd simply followed his heart?

"Hey." She set down her coffee cup.

He blinked the past away. "Sorry. Just…thinking."

"About something much too sad, I'm guessing." Her smile did not reach those eyes that changed depending on the light—from blue to green to hazel, and back to blue again. "Don't be sad," she whispered.

"I hope you two found everything to your liking." Ruby Satterfield smiled down at them.

Kenzie nodded. "Thank you, Ruby. It was wonderful. The meal, the service—all of it was excellent."

"That's what I like to hear. More coffee?"

"No, thanks. One cup was exactly right."

"Fair enough." Ruby granted them a regal nod. "I will be right back." She bustled away and reappeared a moment later. "Satterfield's famous crème brûlée," she announced as she set the tempting dessert in the middle of the table and handed them each a spoon.

The shared dessert was the perfect ending to a wonderful meal, Kenzie thought.

The mood lightened as they jockeyed for bites of the creamy treat. Finn talked about coaching, about how the Titans were shaping up. She loved to see his excitement at building the home team and found herself totally charmed by him—which was why, she reminded herself, that she needed to keep a tight rein on her emotions around him. This more mature, more perceptive Finn could be dangerous to her wounded heart.

But it wouldn't be a problem, she promised herself as she claimed the last spoonful of custard and caramel. She'd learned the hard way—first from Finn, and now, from Tate—that getting too wrapped up in a man simply wasn't for her.

Most of all, she longed for a family of her own—and at last, when her baby came, she would have the family she'd always wanted.

Finn asked, "So how are your folks?"

"They moved to Phoenix five years ago. And then two years ago, they called it quits."

He blinked in surprise. "They got divorced?"

"Yep. Dad moved to Southern California. Mom stayed in Arizona."

"I can't believe it," said Finn. "They were always affectionate with each other. They loved each other and you and their little shop." Sally and Dick Osborne had owned Sally's Gifts and Sundries right there on Central Avenue. "They used to finish each other's sentences and laugh at the same jokes. They were just so…solid together."

"They *were* solid—at least, back when you knew them. From what my mom told me, once they retired, they just kind of drifted apart. Nowadays, I don't talk to my dad all that often, but he calls at Christmas and on my birthday. Mom and I keep in pretty close touch, though. She's got two dogs, a cat and a boyfriend—and she loves helping out at her local humane society."

"Well, as long they're both happy—your folks, I mean…"

"They are, at least as far as I know. Mom's planning to come stay with me for a few weeks when the baby arrives."

"That's good. I always liked your mom."

"And she likes you."

He sat up straighter. "Likes? Present tense?"

"Absolutely. She called yesterday. I told her you were back in town selling houses and coaching the Titans. She predicted a winning season."

"Your mom…" He seemed thoughtful all of a sudden. "Always kind, never judgmental."

Kenzie felt pleased that he remembered her mom so fondly. "Yeah. My mom's the best, no doubt about it."

For a long, sweet moment, they simply stared at each other. Kenzie felt a hint of the old magic they used to share—more than a hint, if she was being honest with herself.

But it was no problem. She liked him and she admired him.

And he'd been so great that day last spring, when he followed her into the Grizzly and made her feel better about everything. Plus, she loved the excitement and focus he brought to his plans for building the home team.

He was a good guy and she was really happy that they were becoming friends—and that was all. Friends. Nothing more.

To keep things from getting too personal, she asked him about football practice.

He said, “It’s intense right now, getting ready for the first game of the season. It’s great watching the team dig in and work hard. Yeah, it’s unlikely we’ll be winning the championship this year, but—”

“*What?*” she said, cutting him off. “Don’t let anyone else ever hear you say such a thing!” she whisper-shouted. “Of course, you’ll win the championship this year!”

“Whoa, Kenzie! Tell me what you *really* think.” He winked at her.

“I think you’re going all the way this year.” She glared at him across the booth. “Now, say it back to me like you mean it.”

“Hmm. Well, let me put it this way—I do intend to give it one hell of a try.”

Finn could have sat there in that booth across from Kenzie straight through to the next morning. They had so much catching up to do.

But how would Ruby Satterfield make a success of her new restaurant if the customers hung around indefinitely? He picked up the check and they thanked their hostess for a terrific meal.

Outside, the warm evening had cooled a little. They strolled along Central Avenue under a slowly darkening sky. Too quickly, they reached her street, and from there it was only a minute or two until they were walking up her front steps.

“Thank you, Finn.”

"Anytime." He was kind of hoping she might invite him in.

But she only smiled again and whispered, "Good night."

As he climbed into his crew cab and headed for his place, the past felt so close. He remembered everything about his senior year with perfect clarity…

He would never forget the homecoming game. The Titans won it 35–6.

And then, the next night, he took Kenzie to the homecoming dance. He was king, Kenzie was queen. She wore a red silk dress and they danced every dance.

They were inseparable, he and Kenzie, all through senior year. They used to sneak off to be alone together in his old Ford pickup. It took flexibility, a lot of it, and determination, too—making love with their clothes half on and half off, trying not to bang their elbows or knees on the steering wheel.

Those were good times. Nothing got him down back then. Not his father's constant carping at him to be the best no matter what. Not the never-ending warnings that he needed to be careful, that he was too wrapped up in Kenzie, that he had his future to think about and he was too young to waste focus on a girl.

He'd ignored most of the crap that came out of the old man's mouth. The way he saw things then, he was going to have everything—the girl he loved and football, too. The future was his. Nothing could stand in his way. They might end up at different colleges, he and Kenzie, and that would be fine. They would make it work long-distance.

He'd been eighteen and unbeatable. He and Kenzie

were forever. They weren't like other people. Nothing could tear them apart—

And then they were having a baby and he was terrified—of the responsibility of trying to be a father. He was terrified and hoping he could do better than his own dad. He obsessed over how they would manage. He considered just quitting football and getting a damn job.

And then the baby was gone and…

All he'd wanted then was to get away, start out fresh, forget all the hard emotions he didn't know how to deal with…

Suddenly, a rabbit darted across the pavement in front of him, breaking into his memories. Finn hit the brakes and the rabbit hopped off into the tall grass on the far side of the road.

Blinking the past away, he reminded himself to focus on the road ahead. He wasn't some crazy-in-love, high-school kid anymore. His big dreams were behind him and the woman he'd once loved was having some other guy's baby…and doing it on her own.

Life could really surprise a man. Sometimes in ways that made him wish things had turned out differently.

But, hey. He'd had a great evening with the girl he'd never forgotten. He sold real estate now and he did a damn fine job of it. And he was going to do everything in his power to get the Tenacity Titans in shape to play serious ball this season.

Finn rolled down all the windows, cued up his favorite country playlist and sang along as he drove home.

For the rest of that week, practice was nonstop action and full contact. Finn worked the team hard. He tried to keep his goals realistic, but his players were improving by leaps and bounds. He had a damn good quarterback in Remy O'Dare, whose dad owned O'Dare Auto Repair there in town. As for the rest of his prospective starting lineup, those boys were beginning to look a whole lot like a real team.

He had to keep reminding himself not to get cocky. This team he and Barrett had put together worked hard, but they weren't tested. They needed time and they were only going to get so much of that before the season opener. Finn knew damn well he was already getting too invested in the success of the Titans. The more he worked with these kids, the more he *wanted* them to kick ass. And maybe he overestimated what they could do.

One thing was for sure, every day was a whole new adventure. He was loving it. It raised his spirits even higher to see his favorite nurse first thing in the morning, with her baby bump stretching the front of her sports-themed scrubs and that smile of hers that could make the darkest day bright.

He got a real kick out of Oscar, too. The kid knew football and he had no hesitation when it came to offering advice. Finn found it humbling, to get regularly schooled on the history of the game and the progress of his players by a brilliant sixteen-year-old. Finn listened to Oscar, anyway. After all, the kid was usually right.

Friday, after practice, Kenzie was on her way to her car when Finn called her name.

She paused a few feet from her Bronco and turned. "Coach Monahan, what can I do for you?"

He jogged up wearing a sly smile. "I think I deserve a reward."

She was grinning, too. "A reward for what, exactly?"

He pretended to think about her question, scrunching his eyebrows together and pressing his lips into a flat line. "For patience. And restraint."

"You? Patient?"

"Yeah. Think about it. It's been days since our dinner at Satterfield's."

"Right." She collapsed the handle of her medical bag and clicked open the Bronco's liftgate. "Three whole days, if you include today—and what is this reward you think you deserve?"

"I like hanging out with you. I think we should do it again."

That made her smile—a giant, beaming sort of smile.

Friends, she reminded herself, frowning now. She and Finn were friends. Their tragic teenage love affair was long over and she needed to remember that.

"Kenz?"

"Hmm?"

"What happened? What'd I do? One minute we're joking around, and then you blast me a smile like I've made you the happiest girl in Montana. And now, you're looking miserable. Why do I have the feeling you're going to jump in your Bronco and burn rubber all the way home just to get the hell away from me?"

He was right. About all of it. She decided to go ahead and tell the truth. "I still…like you. Maybe too much."

One thick, sandy-brown eyebrow hiked up. "Why does liking me have to be a bad thing?"

"I just don't want to…get involved with anyone, you know?"

"Too late." He was grinning. "We're already involved."

She fell back a step. "No. We agreed that we could possibly be friends, but we're not—"

"Yes, we are."

She tried not to roll her eyes. "Excuse me. I didn't even get to finish my sentence."

"Sorry. Continue."

"I…" She groaned. "Now, I have no idea what I meant to say."

"That's okay."

"Hah. To you, maybe—and I remember now. I was going to say, once again, that we are most definitely *not* involved."

He stepped closer. She should probably fall back another step. But she didn't. And then he said in a low, teasing tone, "Kenzie, we're *already* friends and that means we're involved…in a friendship. Get over it. I swear I'm not asking you to marry me."

She glared up at him, defiant. And he just looked at her, waiting. The seconds crawled by. She began to feel a little bit foolish. "Well. Just as long as we're not *more* than friends…"

He pulled his hand from the pocket of his team jacket, plucked off his Stetson and clapped it to his broad chest. "We've known each other for years. We were in love once. We used to tell each other everything. Yeah, it all went to hell. But then we met up again last spring."

"Where are you going with this?"

"Be patient. I'm getting there."

She stifled a smile. “Fine. Continue.”

He said, “It was real, that day last spring. I thought so anyway…”

“Fair enough,” she agreed. “It was real.”

He frowned. “True, things got messed up for a while there after that—all my fault. I own it. But we worked it out. And ever since then, it’s been good, Kenz. We’re honest with each other. We talk about things that matter, and you know exactly what I mean by that. We talk about the things you talk about with a good friend, a longtime friend. The kind of friend who knows you deep down. So, yes, we are *involved* because we’re longtime friends with history who know each other all too well.”

Was her mouth hanging open? She shut it and gulped. “Fair enough then. We’re…*involved*.”

“That’s what I wanted to hear.” He put his hat back on and adjusted the brim. “Let me give you a hand.” Grabbing her medical bag, he stashed it in the back of the Bronco and shut the liftgate. “So here’s the deal. I’ve got to give a speech tomorrow at the Dinosaur Center. I would like to bring a friend. You. Will you go with me?” By then, he actually looked nervous.

She wanted to grab him and hug him, and promise that it would all work out great. “Why are you nervous? You know, everybody in town loves you. You’re the hometown hero.”

He actually winced. “Yeah, that’s what they’re calling it.”

“It?”

“The series of events at the Dinosaur Center—including the event tomorrow. They’re calling the whole thing The Hometown Heroes Series.”

Suddenly, she understood. "Right. It's all about leaders in the community talking about the work that they do."

"Exactly," he said glumly.

"So why the attitude? In case you haven't heard, it's a *good* thing to be considered a hero."

"We both know I'm no hero." His words surprised her.

"I don't get it," she said. "Back in high school, everybody called you a hero and you ate it up."

"Yeah, well. I had an ego the size of the Anaconda Smoke Stack back then. I also had a whole lot to learn. Just because a guy can play football, that doesn't make him a hero."

"Maybe not," she replied. "But stepping in to help out the home team, inspiring a bunch of kids who didn't win a single game last year to shoot for the moon, giving everyone in town something to root for—Finn, those things matter. If people want to call you a hero, let them. And then knock yourself out to prove them right."

He was silent for several awkward seconds. Finally, he muttered, "That was beautiful, what you just said."

"Great. Then do it. Prove them right."

He nodded. "I'll try."

"And tell me the truth…"

"About what?"

"How come you waited until now to ask me to go with you tomorrow?"

He hesitated. But then he shrugged. "I was afraid you'd say no. It took me this long to work up the nerve."

"The great Finn Monahan nervous about asking a woman to spend an afternoon with him? Please."

"Think about it, Kenzie. We have all this history together and you've grown up to be very…independent. Plus, you turned me down last spring, remember?"

She pressed her palm to the swell of her belly. "You know why I turned you down last May."

"Yeah." He looked so solemn right then. "But we've gotten past that. We know where we stand with each other now."

Still, she hesitated. Was she becoming too…attached to him? It did kind of feel that way. Should she say no? "I have a question."

He looked at her steadily. "You're stalling—but go ahead, ask away."

She almost smiled. Because he read her so well. "Where, exactly, will you be speaking?"

"The outdoor amphitheater beside the Dinosaur Center. Eventually I think it's going to be part of the amusement park, but for now it's great for town events," he said. "That's where I'll be giving my talk. And I could really use a friend there for moral support."

"Oh, come on. Everyone in town is your friend."

"Kenzie." He gave her that look, the one she remembered from all those years ago. The one that said, "Quit messing with me and help me out here."

She kind of wanted to hug him. But that could so easily become a habit. "Sure, Finn. I'll be there."

He let out a long, slow breath. "Finally. I'll pick you up at noon. I'm scheduled to speak at one. There will be schmoozing afterward. I'll need you for that, too. It shouldn't be hard. Just stand close to me and look at me like I'm the hottest guy you ever met."

She had to press her lips together to keep from laughing out loud at that last bit. “So really, I'm your date. That's what you're telling me.”

He narrowed those sky-blue eyes at her. “Let me put it this way. Yes, we are *friends.* And yes, you will be my date tomorrow. Both of those statements are true.”

She considered stalling some more, just to give him a bad time. But then again, she'd probably given him enough grief for one afternoon. “Okay, Finn. Pick me up at noon. I'll be ready.”

Chapter Three

When the doorbell rang exactly at noon the next day, Kenzie was standing at the mirror that hung on the back of her bedroom door.

What she saw had her scowling at her own reflection. She definitely looked pregnant. Her boho-cowgirl maxi dress with its tiered crinkle skirt and off-the-shoulder top did very little to disguise her baby bump.

Not that she was really trying to hide anything. Not anymore. Because she was now six months pregnant and the cat, as they say, was out of the bag.

People in town looked at her with warmth and understanding. One or two of her friends had said rude things about Tate. But they all took extra care to make it clear that they were on her side. Several had come right out and offered to help out anytime she needed them.

She frowned at her reflection again. Mostly, she loved being pregnant. She felt curvy and lush. Best of all, her growing belly meant that she would be a mom. Sometimes, though, she missed her flat stomach, her perky breasts and her trim ankles. For the next few months, she was only going to get bigger.

Sometimes lately she did kind of wonder how it would

have been if things had worked out differently with Tate, if she had him to count on now and after the baby came.

But no. She pulled her shoulders back and winked at her reflection in the mirror. Tate was long gone. And she and her baby would manage just fine.

The doorbell buzzed again. She adjusted her top, smoothed a hand down the front of her tiered skirt and went to answer.

Finn greeted her with a grin. "What took you so long?"

She stared at him, deadpan. "Tell me. Does this outfit make me look fat?"

His grin disappeared. "Anything I say right now is going to be wrong—am I right?"

"Probably. But answer the question, anyway."

He drew in a slow, cautious breath. "Here goes. You. Look. Gorgeous."

She laughed then. And it felt good. "Right answer." Stepping over the threshold, she pulled the door shut and then took his arm.

When they arrived at the Dinosaur Center, Mayor JenniLynn Garrett was right there waiting, hand outstretched, to greet Finn and Kenzie.

Finn liked JenniLynn. She was smart and warmhearted. She chatted for a moment with Kenzie, thanking her for her work looking after the students at Tenacity High.

"And not only that," JenniLynn added, "school hasn't even started yet, but you're right there on the field ready whenever the Titans need you. We are so fortunate to have you." She asked when the baby was due and said she'd be checking in regularly, making sure Kenzie was feeling well. JenniLynn added, "You need a hand, you have my number. Use it."

"Thanks so much, JenniLynn. I will."

Next, the mayor turned her sunny smile on Finn. She said what great things she'd heard about his progress with the Titans and thanked him for agreeing to speak today about his growing-up years in town, his life in the NFL and his plans for the team.

Brent Woodson stepped up when JenniLynn was through. He greeted Kenzie and shook Finn's hand. "You already know how glad I am that you let Barrett and me hound you constantly until you gave in and agreed to coach the Titans this year. Thanks, man."

Finn chuckled. "What choice did I have? You two just wouldn't quit."

"Hey. A man's gotta do what a man's gotta do. Now, how about a tour?"

"We can't wait." Finn captured Kenzie's hand and tucked it into the crook of his elbow. She gave him a look that seemed a bit wary, but also indulgent. He grinned at her and then nodded at Brent. "Lead the way."

As Brent charged ahead, he swept out a hand. "You have to admit, it's a nice spot for a tourist attraction."

Finn had to agree. Wooded areas were few and far between in this part of Montana, but cottonwoods and pines surrounded the center. Off in the distance, the low humps of the mountains looked like shadows against the clear, late-summer sky.

Brent showed them the three-story cement education center that housed the recently discovered dinosaur bones. There was also the completed open-air amphitheater, where Finn would speak today, and a large, open space that would eventually become the Dinosaur Park, and offer rides and other dinosaur-themed attractions.

Today, local merchants had set up booths outside the amphitheater, where they sold souvenirs, drinks and food. Surrounding the booths were plenty of picnic tables.

As soon as Brent wrapped up the tour, he led them into the amphitheater, where Kenzie gave Finn's arm a squeeze and went off to sit with a couple of her colleagues from the high school. Finn met Mayor Garrett at the steps leading up to the stage.

"Wait right here until I introduce you," she told him. Then, after giving him another of her dazzling smiles, she mounted the steps to stand behind the stone podium center stage. Once she got there, the lively audience quieted.

She spread her arms wide. "Good afternoon, everybody! I have to say, it means a lot to see so many good friends here."

There was an enthusiastic swell of applause. Jenni-Lynn thanked them for coming. Finn remained by the stage steps as the mayor spoke about the Dinosaur Center and the amusement area that would be opening down the line.

It wasn't long before she glanced down at Finn. "We have a special speaker today, one of our favorite hometown heroes." And then she waved him forward. "Finn Monahan, get on up here!"

Everybody started clapping then. There were whistles and some stomping. More than one voice shouted, "Yay, Coach!"

Finn joined the mayor at the podium, where he got his first real look at the size of the crowd. It seemed to him that the whole town had turned out for this…and then some. The sight of all those faces, so many of them familiar to him, had him feeling downright sentimental.

JenniLynn announced, "I'm leaving you guys in good hands. Finn, they're all yours." She headed back down the steps as the applause swelled again.

Finn waited for the din to subside before gulping away the knot of emotion that had somehow lodged in his throat. Once he knew he could speak without choking up, he called out, "I have to tell you, Tenacity, you are lookin' good!"

Everybody began clapping again. There was more whistling and stomping. He scanned the seats for Kenzie. And there she was, her long hair shining in the sun, wearing a smile so big and bright that it lit her up from inside. She gave him a nod, the same nod she used to give him at the beginning of every game way back in the day, when they were each other's forever love and the Titans couldn't be beat.

And then, he began to speak.

He reminisced about his years at Tenacity High, about all the people who had helped him, the friends and fellow players who had been right there beside him as the Titans went all the way to two state championships. He talked briefly about college and life in the NFL. His gaze kept pausing on faces he saw every day now at practice—Darren Tuttle, Barrett, Oscar Abernathy, the rest of the squad and the staff, including Kenzie, who beamed up at him almost the way she used to, as though he really was some kind of hero.

He talked about Tenacity, about how their town had been through a long, tough time. But things were looking up now.

And he was honored, he said, to be asked to speak today. Honored to be part of a whole new start, grateful to bear witness to a dying town coming back to life. He considered himself privileged, he said, to be coaching the Titans now, watching the team working so hard, gaining skills and confidence day by day. He felt so fortunate to be right there to see how it was done when a community worked together to turn things around.

"I see good times ahead," he predicted. "Everywhere I turn, I see Tenacity growing. Prospering. And I know who made that happen. I know who deserves the credit. You do! Every single one of you.

"So I want to thank you all," he said at last. "You make me proud. And it is so good to be home!"

Kenzie rose to her feet along with everyone else as the amphitheater erupted in thunderous applause. There were shouts and more whistles. People hollered Finn's name and someone yelled out, "You tell 'em, Finn!" Kenzie was whistling, clapping and laughing out loud along with everyone else at the sheer joy of the moment.

Right then, the past was all around her—the good, the bad and all the rest. She put her hand on her big belly and felt pure gratitude…for everything. All of it. The dreams come true and the failures, too.

Because, yeah, things got bad sometimes. But with a little heart, a lot of faith and the determination to start again and make it work this time, what had been broken could be made whole once more.

Eventually, as the amphitheater cleared out, she worked her way down to the base of the stage. She wasn't there long before Finn came to get her.

She took his arm. "You were amazing."

"You're the amazing one." His eyes were so soft. She thought of their teenage love, so sweet and true. No, it hadn't lasted. But it had been beautiful all the same. "I'm real glad you're here," he said, his voice sandpaper-rough.

She almost went on tiptoe and pressed her lips to his.

But she caught herself just in time. Her heartbeat roaring in her ears, she played it super casual. "So…time to schmooze?"

He nodded. "Stay close like you promised."

"You got it. Let's go."

For the rest of the afternoon, she did just what Finn had asked of her. She stuck close by his side and looked at him with something that might have been a little too close to adoration—but only because he'd asked her to.

Or that's what she told herself. Really, it was no hardship playing Finn's adoring date. She liked being at his side.

They visited with their neighbors. And they laughed a lot.

They shared lunch. The Silver Spur Café had set up a booth. And in honor of the Dinosaur Center, the booth offered brontosaurus burgers. Kenzie and Finn each ordered one of those, with fries and icy, delicious stegosaurus shakes.

They joined Oscar and his dad, Jesse, at one of the picnic tables. Kenzie introduced Finn to Jesse. A few minutes later, Barrett and his fiancée, Nina Sanchez, joined them.

Kenzie spotted her friend Lauren Dalton with her twin four-year-old daughters and waved them over.

Lauren and her girls joined the rest of them for a little while. But the cute redheaded twins didn't care much for sitting quietly while the grown-ups talked.

"We'll be back," Lauren promised as she herded them off to get dino dirt cups, which were made with pudding, crushed cookies and candy "dinosaur" eggs. They returned a few minutes later and sat down again.

Kids from the team kept dropping by to talk to "Coach." Finn was good with them, Kenzie thought. He listened when they spoke. His replies were thoughtful and kind…or lighthearted and sometimes funny, depending on the subject.

It would be so easy to imagine Finn as a dad. But Kenzie shook off that thought. Partly because it hurt to imagine the dad he might have been if their baby had survived. And also, well, it was one thing to like kids and know how to interact with them, but quite another to raise them.

And then she almost laughed…at herself. She was hardly an expert on parenting. How could she judge Finn's fitness for fatherhood? Yeah, she had experience with children of all ages. For a couple of years she'd worked in a pediatrician's office there in town, helping to treat kids from birth to age twenty-one. When the pediatrician closed her office and moved her practice to Billings, Kenzie had hired on at the high school. Now, she interacted with teenagers every day.

But that didn't necessarily mean she would be a great mother when her own baby came. Time would tell about that. What she did know was that her little girl would grow up safe and secure in her mother's love.

And as for Finn's potential as a dad, who cared?

It wasn't as if she was hoping to marry the guy or anything. That ship had sailed fifteen years ago.

Finn laughed at something Jesse Abernathy had said and then swiped a french fry off her plate.

She elbowed him in the ribs. "Hey. Get your own."

He put on what she used to call his puppy-dog face, all sad and needy. "I *had* my own but then I ate them all."

"And in what way is this my problem?"

"Share, Kenzie."

She snort-laughed at his pouty face. "You're just looking for trouble."

"I cannot deny it." He leaned closer. "And at least you're smiling now. You looked way too serious there for a minute. What were you thinking about, anyway?"

She fluttered her eyelashes at him. "I'll never tell."

Across the table, her friend Lauren was watching them. Kenzie met Lauren's eyes and mouthed, *What?*

Lauren replied with an easy shrug and a soundless *Later.*

For Finn, the day turned out to be just about perfect—once he got through the speech and the schmoozing. He had a great time hanging out with Kenzie, eating burgers and joking around with friends.

He'd turned off his phone when he left his house and he didn't turn it on again all afternoon. So what if he lost a sale? He had Kenzie at his side and they were just hanging out, being together. The hours sped by much too fast.

They didn't climb back in his pickup until seven that night. Halfway to her house, his stomach growled.

She heard it, too. "What? A brontosaurus burger, fries and a stegosaurus shake not enough for you?" she teased.

"Hey, that was lunch. We haven't had dinner. You hungry?"

"Well, I..." She hesitated. He knew she was thinking that she should ask to be taken home. But the look on her face told him she didn't want the day to end any more than he did.

"How about Mexican?" he offered.

She gave it up. "I could eat a chicken taco or two from Castillo's—I mean, if you're going to twist my arm."

"Consider it twisted." He turned onto Central Avenue and parked in the lot behind the popular restaurant. "Eat in or takeout?"

She met his eyes across the console. "Takeout at my place?"

"Done."

They went in together. Castillo's was packed. They put in their order and stood around by the door until the food was ready, exchanging greetings with friends and neighbors as they came in and went out.

More than one acquaintance stopped to tell him how excited they were for the Titans this year and how much they'd loved seeing him up there on the amphitheater stage at the Dinosaur Center that afternoon.

Kenzie leaned close and whispered, "You're the man of the hour, for sure."

He chuckled, then leaned close and confessed, "We both know I'm a hopeless extrovert, but at this point, even *I'm* getting a little tired of all the attention."

She unleashed a full-out laugh at that, her head tilting back. "Get used to it. It's not going to stop." He wanted to grab her close and kiss her right there in front of half the town.

But, no. She'd made it way clear that they were *just friends*. If he tried to get too close too fast, he would lose what ground he'd gained with her. The ideal would be for her to make the first move.

But was that ever going to happen?

Well, if it didn't, he might be tempted to cross the friends-only line and make the move himself. That would be dangerous. The chances were too high that she'd gently inform him—again—of how she only wanted his friendship and maybe it would be better if they cooled it for a while.

No.

Uh-uh.

He wasn't ready to take the chance of blowing it completely.

Not tonight, anyway. Tonight, they were just good buddies sharing take-out tacos at her place…and maybe honesty, too.

If she didn't want anything romantic with him, at least she might welcome the truth from him. After all, friends should be straightforward with each other—especially *involved* friends, the kind who had history. If he couldn't have her in his arms, he would really like to be able to talk frankly about the past.

At her house, she led him through the living area to the kitchen. They ate at the big oak table in there. He devoured a couple of excellent tacos and chugged half of his Topo Chico Sabores orange soda before he felt ready to bring up the past.

And by then, she was on to him. "Okay." She set down the remaining half of her second taco. "Just tell me. What's on your mind?" She grabbed a paper napkin and wiped the taco sauce from her fingers.

Now that the moment was actually upon him, he didn't know where to start. "Well, I, uh…"

She sipped her red hibiscus soda. He watched her smooth throat move as she swallowed…and still had no clue how to continue.

When he remained quiet, she set down the old-fashioned soda bottle. "This can't be good."

"What do you mean?"

"You look… I don't know, stricken, maybe? And you are never at a loss for words."

He glared at her. Because right then, it seemed easier to get pissed off than to admit how damn nervous he was. "What is that?" he grumbled, pointing at her mouth. "You're grinning. I can't find the words and you think it's funny."

"Well, Finn, that's because it kind of is."

"Right. Twist the knife, why don't you?"

She frowned and leaned closer across the oak table. "Are you actually angry at me right now?" Her voice had turned cautious.

He blew out a hard breath. "Oh, hell, no. I just don't know where to start and I feel like a complete fool, so I'm being a jerk about it."

There was a silence. Finally, she nodded. "Ah."

"*Ah*, what?" he asked, and instantly regretted how impatient he sounded.

"*Ah*, I get it. And it's okay. Take your time. I'm listening."

He almost reached for her hand but thought better of it. This was a confession, not an excuse to cozy up to her. He coughed to clear the tightness from his throat and went for it. "Breaking up with you was the biggest mistake I've ever made."

She sat back in her chair—probably to get some distance between them. Her expression gave him nothing. "The way I remember it," she said in a painfully reasonable tone, "that day you dumped me you said right to my face that you didn't love me anymore."

He hesitated. Suddenly it seemed like a really bad idea to go digging through the ruins of the past. But he'd started this conversation. The least he could do now was give her the unvarnished truth. "Yeah. Well, when I said I didn't love you…"

"What about it?"

"I lied."

"Why?" The single word came out of her mouth on the faintest husk of sound.

"Because I didn't know what to do." He pushed away his empty plate, rested his forearms on the table and folded his hands together. "I thought a new start for both of us would be the best thing. But I couldn't tell you I still loved you and then say I was leaving you anyway. I knew if I said I loved you that you would say it back. And then I wouldn't be able to go."

Her gaze was steady now, holding his. "Your dad," she said flatly. Those two words said it all, but she elaborated, anyway. "He was riding you, pushing you, wasn't he?"

"Kenzie, I—"

She put up a hand. "Never mind. We both know that he was. And I still have more to say."

"Go on, then."

They stared at each other some more. Finally, she continued, "Your dad had all those big dreams for you and he'd made no secret of how deeply he resented me for all the ways I was holding you back, keeping you from moving on and living up to your 'true potential.'" She air-quoted the two words. "He just knew I was going to tie you down. And he must have been so relieved, must have seen my losing the baby as a way to finally get you to leave me behind."

Reluctantly, he gave her the truth. "Yes. All of that is true."

Her eyes were so sad right then. "But still. It wasn't your dad who made the final decision."

"You're right, Kenz. I did. I wanted my big dream as much as my father did."

"And yet you felt guilty about that, didn't you?"

"Yeah." He decided to lay it all out there. "I felt guilty because even though I still wanted you and I really had wanted our baby, I was also relieved that I wouldn't have to try to be a dad *and* a husband while chasing that dream."

"I get it," she said. "I do. I remember how bad you wanted to play pro football, how you couldn't wait to make it to the NFL, to be the starting quarterback for a top team. You used to talk about your dream of winning the Super Bowl, claiming the ring..."

He looked down at his tightly folded hands. "That's right. I wanted it, *all* of it."

"And then I got pregnant and you were stuck..." She

let the words trail off. A long silence followed. What could he say? She was right, after all. She added almost tenderly, "You tried so hard not to resent me."

"I didn't resent you, Kenzie."

"Oh, Finn…" She let out a slow breath and said patiently, "Yes, you did."

"I knew it wasn't your fault. I was the one handling the contraception, after all."

Her grin was suddenly devilish. "And apparently, you were *handling* it poorly."

He pretended to glare her. "Very funny."

And then, her eyes were sad again. "We were only eighteen at the time. We did the best we could."

"I guess you're right."

She tipped her pretty chin high. "We both *know* I'm right."

"Fair enough. And then, after the baby was gone, I just wanted to get away from the guilt and the sadness, to forget our little boy who never drew a single breath. So I said I didn't love you."

Silence echoed between them. He was acutely aware of the decorative clock on the wall across from the table, of the clicking sound it made as it ticked the seconds away. He waited for her to ask if he still loved her, even now.

But she didn't ask. Instead, she set her soft, cool hand on his tightly clasped ones. "It's alright, Finn. I mean that. And I meant what I said that day at the Grizzly. It wouldn't have worked for us. We were too young. All the drama around my being pregnant and then having a miscarriage, the loss and the guilt—it was just too much. It broke us."

There had definitely been drama. He remembered that far too clearly. Including the unbearable family meetings—both families, his and hers. His dad had made those meetings a living hell, yelling at Finn for being "a stone idiot," accusing Kenzie of getting pregnant on purpose to "trap" Finn into marrying her. Once or twice, his dad and Kenzie's dad had almost come to blows.

And then, in the space of a few awful hours one night in mid-July, the baby was gone. Finn hadn't realized how much he wanted that child until there was no child, after all.

Gently, Kenzie squeezed his hands. "We both needed to start over. Yes, I resented you for leaving me. But I also needed time away from you as much as you needed space from me. Every time I looked at you, I would think of our baby, think of losing him. Think of the emptiness where he was supposed to have been. I longed to get away from the reminder of him, of the little boy he never got a chance to be—and yet there you were, the father of the child I would never know. It hurt, it really did, just to be around you then."

He turned his right hand palm up and captured hers. She held on and met his eyes. The look they shared then went on for the longest time. Finally, he said, "I'm so sorry, Kenz."

"Oh, Finn. Me too."

He looked away then. "You're too easy on me."

She squeezed his hand and he met her eyes again. "I don't need to be hard on you, Finn," she said with a sad little smile. "You're plenty hard enough on yourself. And we *were* too young. Too many couples I know went off to college vowing to be true…and then one of them cheated."

"Kenzie, come on. We both know that wasn't us—I mean, yeah, we were too young and we might not have made it as a couple. But I never cheated on you and I never would have done that." She sent him a pained look and eased her hand from his grip. "What?" he demanded. "You don't believe me?"

"I do believe you. But people cheat. You know they do."

He studied her face in search of clues to her real meaning. And suddenly, he *knew.* "You're not talking about college kids. Or about you and me. You're talking about your ex-husband, aren't you?"

Now, she was the one looking away. He waited for her to face him again. Eventually, she did. "Tate's a land man for Treasure State Oil and Gas. I think I've mentioned before that he traveled a lot for work."

"You have mentioned that, yeah."

"Well…" She cleared her throat and then finally continued, "Sometimes, toward the end of our marriage, he'd come back from a business trip and his shirts would smell like somebody else's perfume. Sadly, by then, his cheating was just more proof of what I already knew. It was over. Tate and I didn't want the same things—and as it turned out, we never had."

"What a fool."

She seemed to shake herself. And then, she glanced at the clock.

He got the message. "Had enough of me for one night?"

Her gaze settled on him once more, the corners of her

mouth turning down in a melancholy way. "I didn't say that." He wanted to take her hand again, to offer comfort. But he didn't quite dare. She added, "And, Finn, I did have a great time today."

"Me, too. Thank you for being my date. It was good to have you there with me."

She nodded and then granted him a smile, one that belied the sadness in her eyes. He wondered about that ex of hers. Was she still in love with him?

He really wanted to ask her that question. But before he could work up the nerve to go there, she pushed back her chair.

Finn got the message loud and clear. He'd overstayed his welcome. He rose and fell in step behind her.

She led him to the door, where she turned to meet his eyes again and said almost tenderly, "Finn, I..."

He waited, barely breathing, in anticipation of whatever she might say next. The seconds ticked by and they just stood there, staring at each other. The moment was slipping away from him.

He dared to lift a hand and press his palm to her smooth, soft cheek.

"Finn..." A thrill surged through him as she tipped her face up to him. It was his chance and he seized it. His pulse roaring in his ears, he lowered his lips to hers.

She didn't pull back. Instead, she welcomed him, sliding her arms up over his chest. He felt her sigh against his lips as she whispered his name again. "Finn..."

He gathered her close. And at last he was breathing in the sweet scent of her skin, feeling the roundness at her belly and the fullness of her breasts that brought him sharply to awareness of the baby within her…and also of the whole of her that he'd lost so very long ago.

The kiss took on a life of its own. He breathed her in, his tongue sparring with hers. She let out a soft and urgent little sound.

And then, he lifted his mouth from hers, but only to slant it the other way and get lost in the taste of her all over again. It felt right, as if it was meant to be—to hold her in his arms, to press his lips to hers, to run his hands down her back, feeling the soft shape of her beneath the silky dress she wore.

The past rose up, filling his head with the memory of her in his arms all those years ago, of the kisses they'd shared—so many, some innocent, fleeting. Others long and wet and endlessly deep.

He remembered the way she used to let him in the window of her upstairs bedroom at her parents' house, pushing the window open with aching slowness in order not to make any noise, whispering across the sill at him as he clung to a high branch of the bur oak that grew close to the house.

Shh, Finn. Don't make a sound...

Somehow, he always made it inside without falling and breaking his fool neck. Once he was in, she would lead him to her white cast-iron bed with the pink quilt covered in twining vines and purple flowers, and a mountain of pillows. So many pillows that he would shove half of them to the floor to make room for the two of them, entwined.

"Finn…" She breathed his name against his lips. He marveled that now, tonight, all these years later, he was holding her close in his arms once more.

He thought of how much he'd missed her after he'd walked away from her, of how often he'd had to remind himself that she was lost to him. That he'd made his choice and she would never be his.

Not ever again…

"Finn."

He blinked down at her. "Hmm?"

She pulled away then…but gently. Slowly. "Good night, Finn." She whispered the words like a secret, a covert message for his ears alone.

He said exactly what he was thinking. "I don't want to go."

She gazed up at him, starry-eyed, almost smiling. "Finn…" She was shaking her head. "*Friends*, remember?"

Reluctantly, he nodded. "I get it. I do." He took his hat from the coat-tree by the door and put it on. "'Night, Kenz."

"Drive safe, Finn."

"I will." Smiling now, he stepped out into the gathering darkness.

He drove home thinking how much he wanted to turn his crew cab around and go back.

But he didn't go back.

They were friends and friends only, as she kept reminding him. So shoot him, he found it easy to imagine becoming a lot more than friends with her. He liked her. So much. She'd grown up to be everything he'd always known she would be. Plus, she was even hotter now than back in high school.

Kenzie Osborne was special, no doubt about it. She was the kind of woman who made a man glad he'd had sense enough to finally come home again.

Chapter Four

As soon as Kenzie shut the door, she turned around and sagged back against it.

She'd kissed him…again. And it had been even better than that kiss on Central Avenue last spring. Closing her eyes and resting a hand on her growing belly, she drew a slow, careful breath as she relived what had just happened. She remembered the lovely press of his hard body to her soft one, the feel of his lips on hers…

A silly spurt of gleeful laughter escaped her and she clapped her hand over her mouth. She sounded ridiculous. She was *being* ridiculous.

And at the moment, she didn't even care.

She'd kissed Finn good-night and that kiss had been perfect.

But then later, after she'd changed into a giant sleep shirt, when she stood at the bathroom sink brushing her teeth, she stared into her own eyes in the mirror and watched her face turn beet red.

The kiss had been great. True, it meant nothing. But it had been beautiful, nonetheless.

It was what she'd done before the kiss that bothered her. Before the kiss, she'd overshared in the worst way. The last thing Finn Monahan needed to know was the most pitiful, humiliating truth about her marriage. She'd married a guy who'd not only lied from the first, said he wanted kids when he didn't, but had also cheated.

Repeatedly.

"TMI," she growled and shook the toothbrush at her own beet-red face in the mirror. "Never again."

But later, in bed with the light out, it was Finn's kiss that she remembered. He'd always been the best kisser, alternately tender and possessive, playful and intense.

A long sigh escaped her as her hand strayed downward under the covers.

In the next week, Finn saw Kenzie every day at football practice. When their gazes met, she would smile and wave.

And that was it, the whole of their interaction Sunday through Friday. There was no time for more—not at practice, no way. Not during that particular week. That week, every single second at practice had to be about making the Titans the best they could be. Because Friday night, they would be playing their first game of the season, at home.

As for after practice, well, then there was work. He scrambled to show houses, write offers and close sales. More than once when he finally got home in the evening, he grabbed his phone to check in with Kenzie… and hesitated.

He thought of the previous Saturday night and wondered if she might be thinking about it, too. About the things she'd revealed to him. About that kiss at her front door…

They were getting closer, he and Kenzie. At least it felt that way to him. Did she feel the same?

He realized he was a little bit afraid to find out.

So he never did call her, and she didn't call him.

But he *would* call. No doubt about it. As soon as the Titans won their first game Friday night.

Until then, he was all about the team.

Those boys worked hard. Tenacity was not only the name of their town and their school, but it was also who they were. They got knocked down. But they never gave up.

As each practice went by, Finn felt better about the opening game Friday night.

The Titans would play Bronco Valley High.

Barrett said, "Bronco Valley will definitely give us a run for the money. But our boys are better now than last year, or any year in more than a decade. I'm thinking positive. We just might squeak by with a win."

Finn was thinking the same thing.

Oscar, who had his own system now to organize the stats he loved so much, wasn't so confident. He offered the names of several of the Bronco Valley players who had considerably more skill and experience than the corresponding players on the home team, twisting the knife in his calm, supremely logical way by rattling off performance metrics as well as physical attributes and performance data.

"Numbers don't lie, Coach," Oscar warned.

Finn respected Oscar's analysis of the situation. Last year, the Titans had lost to Bronco Valley by a dismal 55–3. This year, their town and their team were coming back strong. But the hard fact remained that Tenacity hadn't won a game against Bronco Valley since the year Finn headed for the University of Michigan.

Still, Finn had proudly drunk the Kool-Aid when it came to the Titans' chances this year. He was rooting for his boys and he just knew they would come through.

Friday dawned cloudy and cool with no rain in the forecast. Great football weather. At 5:00 p.m., when the team assembled on the field for warm-ups, every player was raring to go. Barrett led them through an easy jog, dynamic stretches, and some light speed and agility drills. After that, they reviewed position-specific walk-throughs and special-team plays.

Back in the locker room before the game, Finn delivered a pep talk and ran down the starting lineup. In the previous week, he'd spoken to each player privately to assign them their positions and explain the reasoning behind his decision. They all knew already whether or not they would be starting. But as tradition dictated, today Finn formally announced the starting lineup to the entire squad.

All the guys seemed pumped. No one was surprised that Remy O'Dare would lead the team as starting quarterback. Remy was tall, lean and smart. He was damn quick on his feet and he had a hell of a throwing arm. On another happy note, middle linebacker Darren Tuttle, son of Rufus the EMT, had made the starting lineup, too.

At the rear of the group of players, Kenzie looked every bit as proud of the team as Finn felt. She sported school colors—maroon scrubs with silver trim—and she rested a slim hand on the proud swell of her belly. When their eyes met briefly, she nodded.

And then quickly glanced away.

* * *

Kenzie loved game night. The energy was palpable, as everyone was excited, ready to cheer the team on.

Yeah, she was a bit annoyed with Finn. She and Finn were supposed to be friends. And shouldn't a friend have called or texted her to check in at least once in the past week?

And was she being absurdly unfair? Absolutely. After all, she could have called *him*.

But she hadn't called him. Because that kiss on Saturday night…

She might as well just be honest about it. Friends did not share kisses like that one.

She needed to stop thinking about that kiss.

But she didn't. Instead, during random moments alone at home, she would find herself idly brushing her fingers against her lips, daydreaming about the exact feel of his mouth touching hers.

"Get a grip, girl," she muttered under her breath.

Because tonight was not about whatever was or was not going on between her and Finn Monahan.

Uh-uh. Tonight, the Titans were playing and she had a job to do.

By kickoff, the bleachers were packed. Kenzie sat on the sidelines not far from the team, her medical bag at her feet, ready to jump into action the moment she was called upon.

In the stands, both sets of cheer squads shook their pom-poms and challenged everyone to "get fired up!"

On the Titan side, tall, burly math teacher Joseph Cutbank roamed the stands. As T-Grizz, the team's mascot, the math teacher wore a surprisingly convincing grizzly-bear costume, one with sharp teeth and wicked-looking claws. Mr. Cutbank also wore a Greek helmet and a shiny maroon cape. In his giant paw, he brandished a double-edged wooden sword painted silver to match his helmet.

T-Grizz backed up the Titans' cheer squad, urging everyone to their feet to shout "Go! Fight! Win!" He also mimed the way they should stomp their feet as they roared, "De-fense! De-fense!" and join in to holler "Score, Titans, Score!" when the offense got anywhere near the goal line.

Truly, Joseph put on a great show. Besides encouraging the crowd, he provided sound effects, alternately growling like a giant bear and letting loose with a battle cry that would have done a Greek warrior proud.

The Titans scored first. What a moment! Tenacity fans—Kenzie included—surged to their feet, shouting and clapping, whistling and stomping. The Titan side of the stands went wild.

But then, the Bronco Valley team took control.

The Titans made it to the end zone a second time, and converted the extra point. They also scored a successful field goal, giving them a final score of seventeen points.

It wasn't enough. When the game clock ticked down to zero, Bronco Valley had triumphed by a score of 27–17.

Finn kept his head up and his shoulders back. He acted proud, smiling and waving, shaking hands with Bronco Valley's head coach. He played it cool and confident. Because it was part of the job to walk tall no matter the final score.

And come on, what was his damn problem, anyway?

What had he expected? He'd known going in that the Titans were unlikely to win, yet the loss had hit him hard.

But why?

It was high school and the team was just pulling itself together. It took time to build a winning lineup, and any coach worth the title knew that.

Didn't matter. Finn was embarrassed. And furious, too.

At himself. He couldn't help feeling that he'd let everyone down, and he entered the locker room expecting to confront a sea of glum, pissed-off faces to match his own.

Wrong.

"Coach!" Darren Tuttle shouted as he pumped his fist in the air. "Titans rule!"

The whole team started clapping then, Barrett included. Finn realized he should say something. Instead, he just stood there with his mouth hanging open, stunned at the totally undeserved applause.

Still, he couldn't deny the proof of his own eyes and ears. Everyone was thrilled. They were high-fiving each other, honestly excited at how well they'd played.

Biff McGuffy, a cornerback, declared, "Two touchdowns! And we only lost by ten." He clapped Finn on the back. "And we will get better, Coach. Just you wait and see!"

Finn was smiling, too, by then. The boys had it right. They'd played their best, and they would only get better from here on out.

He thought of his dad. Finn Sr. only ever counted the wins. And for way too long, Finn had cared far too much about his father's opinions.

Not anymore, he reminded himself for the umpteenth time in the past several years.

Yeah, wins mattered. But so did playing your heart out. These sweaty, cheering guys around him had done just that tonight.

He put up a hand. The locker room fell silent.

"Bronco Valley High took the win tonight," he said. "Those boys outplayed us. But we are just getting started…"

The Titans erupted in shouts of "Yeah!" and "Truth!" and "You said it, Coach!"

Finn nodded. "You guys worked your butts off tonight, and every day for the last two weeks of preseason practice. And take my word for it, you will work even harder. And you will win…and win again. Every setback offers a chance to come back stronger. And you *will* do just that. I know it. And I know you know it, too. Be proud, Titans."

There was whistling and stomping.

Finn couldn't suppress his smile as he reminded them, "And please be on time for recovery practice tomorrow."

Finn was the last to leave the gym that night. And the last person he expected to see as he went out the door was standing in the shadows a few feet away.

"Hey." Kenzie rolled her medical bag closer and stood it upright at her feet. "Good game."

He looked at her sideways. "Bronco Valley would definitely agree."

"The Titans seemed pretty happy with the outcome," she replied.

"I know." He grinned down at her.

"And they *should* be happy, Finn. They did their best. What more can you ask?"

"A hell of a lot." He grinned even wider. "And I will. Just watch me."

She tipped her head toward the dark sky. He followed her gaze. Up there in the heavens, a narrow wisp of cloud drifted across the almost-full moon. "Nice night," she said. At his nod, she asked, "How about some coffee? I even have decaf at my place if you're worried that the real thing will keep you awake."

He studied her upturned face. Her skin glowed in the light of the moon and her changeable eyes were jade green rimmed in deepest blue.

She frowned. "So, that's a no, then?"

He grinned down at her. "Are you kidding? I would love a cup of coffee at your place."

At her house, Kenzie made decaf for both of them and they settled on the sofa in front of the unlit fireplace. She kicked off her shoes and he did the same.

They sipped in silence. In the quiet, Finn could hear the ticking of the antique gold clock on the mantel.

"I don't believe it," he said. "Your mom gave you her precious mercury clock."

She nodded. "She passed it on to me right after she and dad broke up, said that she'd always planned for me to have it."

"It was your grandmother's, right?"

Kenzie nodded. "And my great-grandmother's before her. My grandmother used to tell the story of how my great-granny and her siblings would take the mercury out of the tubes and play with it when they were kids."

"But that stuff is dangerous."

She laughed, a low, husky sound. "Yep. 'It was a different time,' my granny used to say. When my great-granny was a youngster, most people had no idea that mercury could actually harm them."

Finn just stared down at her, smiling. He really did like looking at her, watching her eyes change color and her pretty smile come and go.

"Finn?"

"Hmm?"

"What are you staring at?"

"You. Your eyes always get to me. They change color depending on the light."

"My eyes, huh?"

"Among other things." There was a silence. Neither of them broke eye contact. He was thoroughly enjoying himself.

Finally, she asked in a careful tone, "So then, how are you doing?"

He shifted on the sofa and took another sip of decaf. "In what way?"

She tipped her head to the side. He recognized the cautious look on her face. She was trying to decide how much to say. Finally, she went for it. "Finn, I know how you feel—or how you *used* to feel, anyway—about losing. And tonight, the Titans lost."

He thought of the women he'd dated in the past decade and a half, of how none of them ever really knew him. Because he hadn't let them. But Kenzie knew him all too well. "Yeah," he said. "The Titans lost. And I hate losing."

She made a small sound in the affirmative. "I remember." She knew why, too. But she didn't say it. She left it to him to be truthful. Or not.

"I'm thirty-three years old," he said. "And still, sometimes, I get the feeling that I'm in trouble. That I haven't lived up to my father's expectations, and for that, there will be hell to pay. And that makes me furious."

"Furious at yourself," she added, because she really did understand how his mind worked. "He was pretty awful to you a lot of the time." Her voice was so soft now. She knew that this was an uncomfortable subject for him. It couldn't be a pleasant one for her, either. Finn Sr. had treated her badly, too—even before he learned she was pregnant.

Finn's dad had never approved of Finn's relationship with Kenzie. From the first, the old man had considered her a distraction for Finn. It got a lot worse when his dad learned she was pregnant. And he'd made no secret of his relief when she lost the baby.

Finn tried to think of something good to say about his father. "Hey. At least he never once hit me."

Kenzie wasn't buying it. "Well, except for with words."

"Words don't count."

She leaned a fraction closer. "You don't believe that—or at least, you don't behave as if you do. I've seen you on the field every practice the past couple of weeks, and tonight, too. You never beat up your players with words. You're tough and demanding, but you don't tear them down."

What could he say? She had his number. "You're right. My dad was hard on me. And not always in a constructive way. He's still difficult to deal with, to tell you the truth. I try *not* to be like him."

"Well, you're doing a great job of that." She gave him a teasing smile.

"Thank you."

"So…" She studied his face for a moment. "Back to my original question. How are you doing?" She waited, giving him a chance to reply. When he said nothing, she teased, "You really don't seem upset about tonight's loss, at least not right now."

He chuckled. "I *was* upset at first. Truth is, I was disappointed, and I blamed myself and I was mentally beating up on myself. But then I got schooled."

"By…?"

"The Titans. They're proud of how they played tonight. And they should be. I walked into the locker room and every one of them was smiling. They reminded me of the main lesson I've learned in the past fifteen years. I don't have to live my life by my father's rules *or* his expectations. *I* get to decide what matters to me."

"Wow." She held up a hand and he high-fived it. "Good for you."

They grinned at each other. He wanted to kiss her so bad.

Those shining eyes of hers said she knew it, too. "I've been thinking…"

"About?" he asked.

"About that kiss last Saturday night…"

He braced himself. He knew she would say it couldn't happen again.

But the woman was full of surprises. "Our friends-only rule is ridiculous," she said. "I mean, who are we kidding?"

His breath caught and his heart started racing. Could there be more between them, after all? Or was this the moment she said how she shouldn't have kissed him, that she couldn't trust him to keep his grabby hands to himself? Was this where she said they needed to cool it, that they couldn't be friends, after all?

She met his eyes directly. "I honestly am not looking for a relationship, Finn."

Uh-oh. This was bad. "Got it."

"Me and my little girl, we are a family." She rested her hand on her sweet baby bump. "Just the two of us. I will never count on a man. Not ever again. Do you understand?"

"I do. You've made that very clear."

"I'm not getting married again. Not ever."

"Kenzie, I hear you. I honestly do."

"And you and me, Finn, well..." Her words trailed off. The seconds crawled by as he waited for the ax to fall.

When he couldn't bear it one second longer, he prompted, "Well, what?"

"Oh, Finn. I'm only trying to be honest, to put the truth right out there so we know where we stand with each other."

"Okay," he replied in a low, frustrated rumble. "I get it. So do it. Put me out of my misery, damn it. Say what you're going to say."

She straightened her shoulders. "Alright then. It's like this. I don't want a relationship."

"That's fine," he replied, though it wasn't.

"But it's still there," she added.

He blinked. "What's still there?"

"That…special something, that energy between us."

How the hell was he supposed to respond to that? Should he deny the clear truth of it in the hopes that she'd believe him and not ask him to leave?

No. She knew him too well and she wouldn't believe him. And besides, dishonesty sucked.

So he laid it right out there. "Yeah, Kenz," he admitted glumly. "At least the way I see it, that fire between us? It's hotter than ever."

She nodded…slowly, as though he'd said something much more profound than the simple truth. "We need to stop pretending that there is no fire. We're not kids anymore. We can certainly behave like the adults we are."

Where was she going with this? He'd thought she was just about to show him the door…and she probably was. Then again, she didn't *look* like she intended to ask him to leave. He gritted his teeth and reminded himself not to get his hopes up.

Then she said, "As long as we both understand that we're not going anywhere serious, well, what's the harm?"

"What exactly are you getting at, Kenzie?"

"Uh. Well, I can't help thinking that we could just, you know, play it by ear. Be friends and be honest, and if we end up in bed together…"

He counted to ten slowly as he waited for her to finish that sentence. When he got to ten and she just sat there, looking at him as though she'd made herself perfectly clear, he demanded, "Kenzie. If we end up in bed together, *what*?"

She frowned. "Maybe you're not even interested in

getting intimate with me right now—I mean, in my condition…"

"Kenzie, I *am* interested. Very, very interested."

"Oh." Bright flags of color stained her soft cheeks. "Well, good." A nervous laugh escaped her. She gestured down at her round belly. "So this wouldn't be a problem for you?"

"Nope. Not a problem. What else?"

She made a thoughtful sound. "We would both have to be sure not to get any ideas that it's more than it is."

That didn't sound so good. "You're going to need to clarify that for me."

"I'm saying that if we do end up being lovers, we would, of course, enjoy it for as long as it lasts. But it couldn't last all that long."

"Why is that?"

"It would have to be over by the time my baby's born."

He took a minute to digest that bit of information. "And then what?"

"And then we try our best to remain friends, however it all works out."

Well, that certainly sounded like a disaster waiting to happen. Supposedly, people enjoyed friends-with-benefits arrangements all the time. But how often did they stop with the benefits and still remain friends?

He didn't really want to see the stats on that particular outcome.

She must have read his thoughts by the look on his face because she pinned him with a scowl. "You think it's a bad idea, don't you?"

He hedged. "I didn't say that."

"But you're thinking it, aren't you?"

"No." It was only half a lie. Yeah, becoming lovers again could easily turn out to be a very bad idea. But any chance with Kenzie was better than no chance at all.

"Then what *are* you thinking, Finn?"

"I'm thinking, who knows how either of us will feel about things later? As for right now, though, I am thinking yes! Spending more time with you works for me in a big, big way."

"You mean that?" Her eyes were gleaming now.

"A hundred percent," he confirmed. "We'll see where it goes and we'll keep it honest."

She gave a little cough and added almost sternly, "And we both understand that a ring and a walk down the aisle will not be happening."

They did? Who knew what would happen? He sure didn't. And he would very much prefer to leave things open-ended, see where this little agreement of theirs took them.

But he didn't want to say that. If he did, she just might show him the door in a permanent way.

That couldn't be allowed to happen. Because wherever this was going between them, he intended to see it through.

Tonight, for the first time in years, Finn knew exactly what he wanted from Kenzie. And what he wanted was more than she offered him now—more than he deserved, too, if he was honest.

He believed her when she said she would never get married again, that she and her baby would be a family, just the two of them.

Of course, he believed her. Love hadn't been kind to her. She had no reason to put her trust in a man.

She'd found love twice. Both times, she'd ended up broken-hearted. First, Finn himself had walked away from her, and he'd done it right after they'd lost a child. And then she'd married a guy who lied to her, cheated on her and finally walked out on her, too.

However, tonight, as they sat here on her sofa talking so honestly about the past, about his father's cruelty, about how winning wasn't everything and sometimes what looked like a loss turned out to be the finest sort of victory…

Tonight, right here in her living room, Finn had finally seen the light.

He wanted Kenzie. However he might have her. For as long as it might last.

What she offered him now was so much better than nothing. Whether she knew it or not, her plan gave him hope for a second chance.

"Alright, then," he said. "Let's spend more time together, see where that takes us."

She looked at him sideways. "Are you sure about this?"

"You bet I am. What are you doing tomorrow? Come out to my place for dinner."

Those eyes were more green than blue right then… and very wide. "Tomorrow?" Now, she looked terrified.

Apparently, it was all fine and dandy to dance around the subject of becoming more than friends. But actually moving in that direction scared her. A lot.

He wanted to grab her, pull her close and whisper that she didn't have to be afraid, that he was all grown up now and he would do this right. But that might alarm her all the more. Better to keep it light and easy.

"No time like the present," he replied cheerfully. "After all, if we did become lovers, I'm guessing you would expect it to be over when the baby comes."

"Hmm." She frowned. "Probably several weeks before the baby's due, depending."

"Depending on what, exactly?"

She gave him one of those looks women often give men, a look of great patience mixed with barely masked annoyance. "Finn. Please. There are any number of reasons why a very pregnant woman might not be available for hot, sexy times. You don't really expect me to list them for you, do you?"

"Uh…"

"Be very careful about what you say next," she advised.

He thought he saw a spark of humor in those fine eyes. But he wasn't about to put his observation to the test. "Well, tell me this, then, Kenz. How far along are you right now?"

"Tomorrow, I'll be at twenty-six weeks."

"Then realistically, if we do end up enjoying…benefits, we don't have that much time. We need to get moving on it."

She gave him that look, the one that said he was skating on very thin ice. "Get moving? Really?"

"Yeah. Really. If we don't, then whatever might happen won't happen because it will be too late before we even get started."

For a second or two, she just stared at him blankly… and then she burst out laughing. "You're just messing with me."

He put a hand to his heart. "Never. If I do have a

chance with you I'm going to want all the time I can get. Can you blame me for that?"

She didn't answer immediately. Then she groaned. "Finn, you are impossible."

"Come on. Just work with me here. Dinner. My place. Six tomorrow night." She was shaking her head. For a moment, he felt certain that she would shut him down.

But then she grumbled, "Fine. Six."

He took great care not to look as triumphant as he felt.

Chapter Five

"Big place," Kenzie said when Finn answered the door.

"Big and empty," he replied in that charming, rueful way of his. Like he was kind of embarrassed to be tall, hot…and rich, as well.

"I brought red." She showed him the bottle. "Not that I can drink any. But, hey. It's a nice wine and I assume we're having steaks?"

He took the bottle and stepped back. "Thank you. Come on in."

She crossed the threshold into an enormous great room with wide-plank cedar floors, a fireplace of natural stone and tall windows framing views of the endless prairie and the distant mountains. "It's beautiful," she said. The little furniture he had was expensive, with two giant sofas, a couple of club chairs, a big coffee table and some floor lamps. No rugs. "I remember the family who lived here."

He was nodding. "The Rawlingses."

"Yeah. Fourteen years ago, they sold their business in Seattle and opened a tractor dealership in town. What they hadn't factored in was that Tenacity was already in a slump. When things kept getting worse, their dealership went bust."

He made a thoughtful sound. "I did hear that they had a lot of family money, so I'm thinking they landed on their feet."

"Well, good for them," she said solemnly. "Too many lost too much trying to make a go of it during the tough times." And then, she put on a smile. "On a lighter note, I love what you've done with the place."

"As in…not a thing?"

She shrugged. "You said it, I didn't."

"I'll get there, just you watch."

"I have no doubt."

"And the Rawlingses' loss was definitely my gain," he said. "I got a great price for the property, including the house, the barn, twenty acres and enough furniture to get by for a while."

"You planning on buying a few horses and running cattle?"

"One horse, maybe. Someday. But you know me. I like my Stetson as well as the next guy. At heart, though, I'm a town boy and I sell real estate. I'll leave the cattle ranching to the experts." He swept out a hand. "This way."

She followed him past the wide staircase and into the kitchen, which was as big and impressive as the living room. There were acres of stone countertops and the giant Wolf range had a copper hood to match.

"Ginger ale?" he offered. "Sparkling water?"

"Sparkling water sounds good."

He poured her some fizzy water over ice, opened the wine and served himself a glass. "Real nice," he said with an approving nod.

"Glad you like it." She raised her glass and he tapped it lightly with his.

And then, for the longest time, they stood there at the enormous island grinning, staring deeply into each other's eyes.

Finally, Finn tipped his head toward an archway. "It's nice out. Come on..." She fell in step behind him and he led her past a full-size pantry, a laundry room and the mudroom.

When they reached the back door, he pulled it wide. "After you."

She went onto the covered back deck, where a round cast-iron table was set for two. He had a charcoal cooker going. He must have added mesquite to the coals for extra flavor. It smelled so good. She walked to the edge of the deck and admired the rippling prairie grasses, the big red barn in the distance and the rustic split-rail fencing.

He was standing at her shoulder. She could feel the warmth of him so close.

"Hungry?" he asked.

She turned and smiled up at him. "Lately, I am *always* hungry."

"Well, I'd better feed you, then, huh?"

His eyes always got to her. They seemed to see right down inside her. With Finn, she'd always felt *known*, somehow. And in the best way, too. Because his eyes said he liked what he saw.

And what were they talking about...?

She set her half-finished glass of water next to his wineglass on the iron table. The late-summer wind blew down from the distant mountains. She could hear the soft rustle of the long prairie grasses.

"Kenz?" He said her name so sweet and low, on a whisper of breath.

"Hmm?"

"I'm glad you're here."

She knew what was coming. She could see the intention shining in his eyes and she signaled her eagerness for it with a secret smile and a hint of a nod.

His lips met hers, the softest breath of a touch. She felt the contact like a bolt of lightning, taking her over, lighting her up inside.

He was smiling, too. She could feel that smile against her parted lips and she waited for him to pull her closer.

But he didn't. Instead, he brushed his mouth back and forth across hers.

She gave in first. With a small, hungry cry, she surged up on tiptoe. Sliding her hands upward over his big, hard chest, she clasped his wide shoulders and pressed her mouth firmly to his.

He groaned.

She laughed, the sound low and husky to her own ears as she parted her lips, inviting him deeper.

Now, she was the one groaning as he gathered her closer and kissed her harder. Their bodies were pressed together, her round belly against his belt buckle.

This, she thought. *Finn and me, holding each other, kissing like our lives depend on it. Oh, I have missed this for too many long years...*

She was about to grab his hand, drag him inside and straight to his bedroom…wherever that might be in this mansion of his.

But then, he gently clasped her shoulders and moved back a step.

She blinked and gazed up into his waiting eyes. "What now?"

He looked flushed and way too pleased with himself. "This is going better than I dared to imagine it would."

That made her laugh. How did he do it? He charmed her so easily. She tried to look stern. "Don't get your hopes up, mister."

He smirked. "Hope's not the only thing *up* about me."

She laughed some more, and scolded, "That's not even funny."

"Sorry." He faked a contrite expression. "But you did laugh."

"Okay, fine. It might have been a *little* bit funny."

He was looking kind of serious now. "Am I moving too fast?"

"Yes," she replied. And then she admitted, "Although the truth is, a minute ago I was on the verge of dragging you off to your bedroom."

"Damn. So close." His voice was tender. Lifting a hand, he guided a wind-tossed curl of hair away from her lips and back behind her ear. She felt the echo of his touch even after he'd lowered his hand again.

"So what now?" she asked.

"How about some dinner?"

"I'm in."

"Excellent. I'll put the chicken on and pour you more sparkling water."

"I thought we were having steaks."

"We were. But I gave it more thought and as I recall, you used to love mesquite-grilled chicken."

"And I still do." What she loved even more was that he'd remembered. "Yes, please. Put the chicken on."

* * *

Two hours later, Kenzie had eaten a couple of chicken thighs, a baked potato and a nice big helping of green salad with shaved Parmesan and lemon vinaigrette.

In the distance, cirrus clouds glowed orange and purple, and the sun had sunk below the horizon. After the meal, Finn had cleared the table and offered decaf and rainbow sherbet for dessert.

Now, her sherbet bowl was empty. As for the coffee, she was on her second cup. And aside from her need to visit the powder room soon, she could sit here forever watching the sunset and sipping decaf with Finn at her side.

"This was delicious," she said.

He sat back in his chair. "That's what I like to hear."

"As I recall, when we were together back in high school, nobody cooked in your family but your mom."

"You remember it right. We Monahan men were very busy doing…*man* things. My dad couldn't even be bothered to learn how to use the big grill out back. My mom did everything—around the house, in the yard. You name it, she took care of it."

"You guys had a maid, though, didn't you? I thought that was very fancy the first time I had dinner at your house."

"We had people who came in and cleaned. Sometimes Mom would hire someone to help when we had company for dinner or when there was a party or a cookout. But she was in charge and she did most of the work herself."

"I don't know why, but I thought you helped out around the house."

"Nope. I didn't learn how to make a bed or do laundry until I was in college. At home, I dropped my dirty clothes on the floor of my room and then forgot about them. Within a day or two I would find them, clean and pressed and neatly folded in a drawer or on a hanger in my closet."

"You make your mom sound superhuman."

"She *is* amazing. My brothers and I, though…" He let his words trail off with a shrug before going on. "We were spoiled rotten. Just like my dad. Entitled, that's what we were."

That surprised her. "You never *acted* like you were entitled."

"That's probably because my mom also taught us to be polite, to help out wherever we were needed—except around the house."

She raised her glass to him. "I'm so pleased to see how far you've come toward self-sufficiency."

"Thank you. I'm working on it." He set down his wineglass and rose.

She glanced up at him, grinning. When he offered his hand, she took it. His grip was warm and firm. Hot little shivers slid down the backs of her knees as she stood. "That look in your eyes," she said softly.

"Yeah? What about it?"

"It ought to be illegal."

He wrapped his free arm lightly around her and reeled her in even closer. As he nuzzled her hair, he whispered, "I admit, I just might be getting…ideas."

"Hmm…"

His lips brushed her cheek. "More coffee?"

She elbowed him lightly. "Are you kidding? This baby takes up too much space for another cup of coffee.

There's hardly room for my bladder anymore. What I really need is a quick visit to the powder room."

"For that, I would have to let go of you."

"And I would definitely advise you to do that. Like… now."

"Whoa!" He stepped away. "Come on, I'll show you where it is."

"No need. I spotted it on the way in." She turned on her heel and headed inside.

In the half bath, she relieved her bladder, washed her hands, smoothed her windblown hair and then leaned in to meet her own eyes in the mirror.

"You shouldn't," she whispered to her reflection, noting that her eyes gleamed with anticipation and her cheeks were flushed with excited color. "You like him too much. You always have…"

And really, *liked* was far too bland a word for the emotions Finn Monahan had stirred in her over the years. She had loved him wildly, longed for him desperately.

For a while, she'd believed she hated him…but that was just self-protection. She'd needed to get over him and telling herself she hated him had helped her to move on.

And right now…

Right now, she wanted him. So much. Wanted the magic of his kisses, the sweetness of a love affair…just for a little while. Just a last, wild fling before she settled down to a good life with her baby, to a family of two.

However…

She bit her lip and shook her head at her face in the mirror. It wasn't a good idea.

Not tonight, anyway.

This was happening too fast and she needed to put the

brakes on, give herself a week—or a few more days, at least—before jumping into a love affair, however brief and frivolous. Tonight, she needed *not* to get carried away in the excitement of the moment. She needed to give herself enough time to be sure.

Of what? the voice inside her asked.

There was nothing to be sure of. It was a *fling*—short and sweet and just for fun.

In the mirror, her eyebrows were all scrunched together and she was chewing her bottom lip.

Because clearly, she wasn't ready. "Not tonight," she whispered, drawing her shoulders back, giving her reflection a firm nod. "Not tonight." She pulled open the door and headed through the giant kitchen and the back hallway to the deck.

When she went out the back door, Finn stood at the top of the steps leading down to the backyard that seemed to go on forever, a sea of waving grasses interrupted by the beautiful rustic fences and the big red barn. The whole, wide-open expanse of prairie looked magical in the fading light.

Kenzie paused by the table. He'd cleared it while she was in the house. That made her heart ache a little, made her think of the boy who never did housework, the boy who left his clothes on the floor when he was through with them. The boy whose father had never struck him but instead had hurt him with harsh words and unreasonable expectations.

He turned and gave her that big, open smile of his. "There you are."

She held out her hand to him. In three long strides,

he reached her side. When his fingers closed over hers, all her nerves and anxiety just faded away.

She wanted him. She saw in his sky-blue eyes that he felt the same.

No, it wasn't forever. And that was just great. Forever, after all, had not been kind to her.

He leaned in. She melted against him. Their lips met.

Sheer heaven, she thought—to be with him now, on this warm, late-summer evening as the sky slowly darkened and the full moon rose over the faraway mountains.

When he lifted his head, she sighed and smiled lazily up at him. "Please take me to bed, Finn."

He kissed the tip of her nose. "Done."

His room was right there on the main floor, down a hallway off the great room. It was all in browns and grays with touches of red in the comforter and pillows.

"This is nice," she said, her voice breathless, her body eager to be there with him, held close in his arms.

He dropped a trail of kisses down the side of her neck, leaving heat and longing in his wake. "I like where I sleep to be comfortable."

"I get that."

Lifting his head to look in her eyes again, he added, "So this is the only room I fixed up myself. The bed and night tables are of reclaimed barn wood—red oak."

"It's beautiful."

"Thanks." He gave her a crooked grin. "Why are we talking about the furniture? There are so many more interesting things to get into right now."

"Such as?"

"You." He kissed the word onto her waiting lips.

"Now, come here…" Her feet left the floor as he scooped her up into his arms and headed for the bed. Carefully, he set her down on the edge of the mattress. Then he sank to his knees.

"You are so eager," she observed as he pulled off one of her boots and then the other.

"Eager doesn't begin to cover it." He whipped off her socks. Then, sweeping upright again, he pulled her to her feet and went to work on the long line of abalone shell buttons down the front of her flowy boho dress.

"Finn…"

"Shh. I'm busy."

"That really isn't necessary."

Frowning, he met her eyes. "Huh?"

"Undoing all these buttons. Watch." She sidestepped, grabbed the filmy skirt of her dress and whipped it up and over her head. "Done." She tossed the dress to the nearest chair and stood before him in her bra and panties.

He looked her up and down. "You are so beautiful."

She rested a hand on her stomach. "If you're into pregnant ladies."

His laugh was a low rumble. "I'm into *you*." He reached for her. She happily melted into his arms again. They stood by the bed sharing a kiss that went on and on.

Eventually, he lifted his head. "I have way too many clothes on."

"True."

Dropping to the side of the bed, he yanked off one boot and then the other, removed his socks and rose to his feet again. After that, it took him no time at all to get everything off but his boxer briefs.

She allowed herself a long, slow look from the top of

his head to the tips of his toes. He was bigger, broader than she remembered, a grown man in every way, his thick chest dusted with dark hair, his belly lean and hard. She let her gaze trail downward over the bulge in his briefs and lower. Her eyes lingered on his right knee and the faint scarring there from more than one surgery.

She'd seen the original injury happen, watched in horror as he went down on ESPN for the whole world to see. He'd injured his left knee, an ACL tear that had healed—only to tear again the following season.

A low chuckle rumbled in his broad chest. "Yep. That first injury was the beginning of the end of my NFL career."

"I remember," she said softly.

"I played for six more years. But never at the same level as before. After the fourth time I was traded, I decided I was ready to move on, to try something else."

She met his eyes. "I'm so sorry, Finn. I know how much you loved the game."

"I still love the game," he said. "And I'm thinking the Titans are going to go far." They shared a slow smile. And then, he turned to the bed again and pulled back the covers. "Come here, Kenzie Osborne…" He held out his hand. "Prettiest girl at Tenacity High…"

She went into those big arms eagerly. All her doubts and hesitations forgotten, she happily lost herself in another endless, perfect kiss.

When he pulled her down to the white sheets with him, she went eagerly. He took off her bra. She slid off her panties and dropped them over the side of the bed as he shoved down those boxer briefs.

At last it was just the two of them, Finn and Kenzie,

after all these years. Naked together without bitterness or pretense.

It was the past and yet so very different. He was still the sweet boy she'd loved so long ago…and more, too. He was stronger. Truer, somehow. More sure of himself and also less arrogant.

And so careful, to be gentle with her. To take his time. To look in her eyes and say her name… "Kenzie…"

She whispered his right back to him. "Finn…"

His mouth covered hers. She opened to him eagerly.

Not too much later, on a soft moan of pleasure, she asked, "Who knew this would ever happen?"

"Not me," he said, his voice low and gruff as he buried his head between her open thighs. He looked up. "But I dreamed of it. More than once, too." And he kissed her there again.

She pulled his hair and cried out at the sheer wonder of it. All these years and here they were again.

Kenzie and Finn. Older and wiser.

Holding each other close on a Saturday night.

No, it wasn't love and they both knew it. It was just for now, and that was perfect.

He took a condom from the bedside drawer and rolled it down over himself. When he looked up and saw her watching him, he winked at her. She giggled like she used to do when they were kids.

And then, he settled back against the pillows and reached for her again. Lifting her with his big hands, he guided her to straddle him. She did so eagerly, going up to her knees above him. Slowly, she claimed him, her eyes locked with his as he filled her.

It was so good, just right. She let her head fall back

and her eyes drift closed as she rocked above him. Her long hair trailed down her back, tickling a little, brushing his hands where they clasped her waist.

"So beautiful," he whispered against her parted lips when she bent down to claim him with a kiss.

The rhythm picked up. Her body felt supersensitive, acutely alive. She never wanted it to end.

He said her name again, his tone sweet and low. Then he muttered on a growl, "I am one lucky man."

She laughed at that, a laugh that soon became a moan of pleasure as she curved her body over him. Now, her hair fell like a curtain around them. He reached up under the long strands and caught her face between his hands. "So beautiful… So right…"

Their lips met again. She opened for him on a low, hungry groan. He gave her a long, deep kiss as he carefully guided her down to the bed again, turning them both so they were on their sides facing each other. His big palm skated over her right breast. She moaned at the sweet pressure.

His fingers strayed downward over the bulge of her belly. For a moment, she thought of her baby, sleeping there, of Finn's big hand brushing close to the life growing within her.

His touch was soothing. And warm. She sighed at the comforting feel of it.

He laid his palm on the swell of her hip. And then, clasping her thigh, he guided her to wrap her right leg around him. She took it from there, pressing her hips tightly against him, feeling him slide deeper inside.

They both groaned at that.

She pulled back just enough to meet his eyes and to give him a slow, knowing smile.

"Come back here," he commanded, his voice gruff with need as he wrapped his hand around the back of her head and took her mouth again. This time, his kiss was hard and deep.

By then, her body was on fire, burning up with light and heat. She hovered on the edge of completion.

He put his mouth to her ear, caught her earlobe gently between his teeth and worried it. She cried out, a lost, ecstatic sound. He gave her earlobe another quick nip. And then he claimed her lips again.

"Finn..." She breathed his name against his mouth as he commandeered another long, endless kiss. Swept away on a wave of pleasure, she rocked into him, faster now, frantic.

He whispered things against her parted lips, lovely things—that she was beautiful, that there was no one like her, that he couldn't get enough of her, that she took his breath away.

She believed those things as he said them. They thrilled her in that moment, though she was a grown woman now, one who knew not to put too much faith in the lavish things a man might say when he holds a woman naked in his arms.

But for now, she set her wariness aside. The things he said were lovely. They were absolutely perfect, exactly what she needed—to feel beautiful and adored, just for tonight. It felt decadent and delightfully self-indulgent, sharing dinner and pleasure with this beautiful man who had once been the boy that she loved.

Groaning her name against her throat, he surged

tightly into her. She felt him go over, felt him pulsing within her, his big arms tight and hot around her.

All rational thought fled as her body took its cue from his. She felt only joy as her climax shimmered through her, hot and bright as a shooting star streaking through the clear night sky.

Chapter Six

Finn didn't want Kenzie to go.

But he knew that she *would* go. She had that look. Vulnerable…and a little bit rattled.

Tonight had been spectacular—for him, anyway.

But she'd told him more than once that she wasn't looking for a real relationship. Being friends and temporary lovers was about as far as she would go.

He was holding her close, right there in his bed, feeling absurdly, deliriously happy, when she whispered, "I should get going."

He kissed the tip of her pretty nose. *Stay...* The word was right there, pushing to get out.

But he didn't say it. Her eyes had already answered that question and the answer was no.

So they got up. He pulled on his jeans as she collected her scattered clothes and put them on.

"Thank you," she said softly when they stood together at the front door. "The dinner was amazing and—" her big eyes were locked with his "—so are you."

Damn. He wanted…

A whole bunch of things she wasn't going to give him. At least not right now.

And if he hoped to have a prayer for any kind of a

chance with her, he was going to have to be careful not to crowd her. She had that look—hungry for more. And also absolutely unwilling to admit it.

If she wouldn't stay tonight, would she say yes to getting together tomorrow?

Yeah, big guy. Good luck with that.

He tried, anyway. Because she needed to know what he wanted even if she wasn't going to give it to him. "Come on back over for breakfast in the morning," he said.

Her eyes lit up…and then she looked down. He waited. She seemed to be studying the toes of her boots. At last, she lifted her gaze to him again. "The thing is, I have a lot of stuff at home I should take care of."

He only smiled and said mildly, "Okay, then. See you at practice Monday."

"Absolutely."

He wanted to kiss her. And she was staring up at him as though waiting for something. He hoped it was a kiss, so he went for it, settling both hands lightly on her shoulders and then bending close.

She neither turned away nor pulled back. He took that as permission. Slowly, carefully, he covered those soft lips with his. She sighed. He pulled her closer. As he deepened the kiss, all he wanted was never to let go.

But he did let go. And then he opened the door for her. Somewhere out in the dark, crickets chirped and a night bird let loose with a sweet trill of song. "Monday," he said.

"See you then."

He watched her walk down the front steps and along

his front walk to her waiting SUV. Two minutes later, with a last wave out her open window, she drove away.

The next morning, he was standing at the kitchen window staring blindly out at the waving grasses and the pretty red barn when his phone buzzed with a text. It was Kenzie.

I really did have a wonderful time last night.

Nine words. They made him bold. So, then. Breakfast?

He held his breath as he waited for her answer. Finally, the words appeared.

It's Sunday. Nothing's open.

Now, he was grinning. Come here to my place. I'll cook breakfast. Hardly daring to breathe, he waited for her answer. Several endless seconds struggled by. He just knew she was framing excuses.

But then, she wrote: My turn to cook. Can you be here in twenty?

He grinned at the phone in sheer happiness. On my way.

Kenzie planned to feed him, maybe visit for a while over second cups of coffee...and then send him on his way. She honestly had the best of intentions.

But then, she pulled open her door and found him standing there on the welcome mat. He wore faded jeans, rawhide boots, a Western shirt, a tan Stetson and a grin that managed to be both devastating and kind of shy.

Just the sight of him had her thinking of last night, of his big bed and his warm hands, his kisses that used to drive her wild as a teenager…and still did as a grown woman.

Go for it, whispered a yearning voice inside her head. The days were flying by. She would hold her baby in her arms in no time.

Why waste a minute? she couldn't help thinking. They were in this now and it wouldn't last forever.

He swept off his hat. "Hey…"

Melting inside, she grabbed his arm, pulled him over the threshold and shoved the door shut.

His breathtaking smile got wider and those sky-blue eyes made promises she intended to make sure he kept—and before breakfast, too. "Glad to see me?" he asked.

She moved close enough to put her hands on his chest. "Call me shameless," she advised.

"Happy to." Eyes locked with hers, he stuck out an arm and hooked his hat on the coat-tree there by the door.

She kissed him. Because she wanted to. Because it felt so good. Because by then, he had wrapped both strong arms around her. And because the way he looked at her made her feel like the most beautiful woman on Earth, a woman both fascinating and deeply desired.

When she sank back on her heels, she grinned up at him and asked, "So exactly how hungry are you?"

"Is this a trick question?"

His shirt had snap buttons. She fiddled with the top one. "I just want to know how soon you need to eat."

He lifted a hand, caught a lock of her hair and rubbed it between his thumb and the tips of his fingers. "I have an idea…"

"Oh, do you, now?"

He nodded. Slowly. And then he slid one arm behind her back and the other behind her knees and lifted her off the floor. "Let's discuss this in your room."

She wrapped an arm around his neck and laid her head on his shoulder. "Okay," she whispered. "Let's do that."

"Kiss me," he commanded.

She kissed him. And kissed him again.

And then, he carried her to her room, set her down on the turned-back bed and sat beside her. She toed off her sandals and watched as he took off his boots and socks.

The past—*their* past—was so close right then, or so it seemed to her. She still remembered their first kiss. It had happened under the bleachers during freshman year after the second game of the season. He'd been shy and so had she. Their teeth had knocked together and they'd both jerked away.

She remembered her own embarrassment and how wide his eyes were, the way he'd whispered desperately, *Kenzie, I'm so sorry...*

He bumped her shoulder with his. "What is going through that mind of yours?"

She bumped him back. "Our first kiss."

He groaned. "Anything but that."

"Oh, come on. We were adorable."

"Kenz..." He kissed her and she kissed him back. It felt so good, so right, the two of them, just sitting here, kissing and then kissing some more.

Eventually, in the middle of yet another, slow, tender, perfect kiss, they fell back across the mattress. That kiss went on for quite a while. When it ended, they were lying on their sides. She stared at him, grinning, and he crossed his eyes.

"Oh, stop." She whacked him lightly on the shoulder the way she used to do when they were at Tenacity Elementary and he would chase her around the playground and then stick his tongue out at her when he caught her. "Grow up," she grumbled.

"What fun is that?" he teased. And then he was kissing her again, so sweetly at first, but then deeper, harder.

Finally, she framed his face between her hands. "Finn…"

"What?"

"Everything off. Now."

They were both naked in a matter of seconds. He grabbed his jeans, pulled a condom from a pocket and set it on the nightstand.

She sat in the center of the bed, arms crossed over her ever-expanding middle, staring up at him, thinking that he was the finest-looking man she'd ever known, bar none. "We should talk."

He gulped. "About?"

"Protection. Do you always use a condom?"

"Yes, I do. Every time, except for you and me way back when…"

She smirked up at him. "Learned your lesson, did you?"

"Yep."

"As an RN, I'm an enthusiastic supporter of safe sex."

He looked slightly pained. "Okay…"

"However, in this case, I think we're good to go without the condoms. I mean, I'm already pregnant. And I got tested after I found out what my ex had been up to. Tate's a cheater, but he didn't give me any diseases."

"Alright." Finn stuck the condom back into the pocket of his jeans and rejoined her on the bed. Wrapping her up in his warm arms, he guided her down to the pillows.

She gazed up at him, amazed to be here in her own bed with him. Until very recently, she never would have guessed such a thing could ever happen.

But it had happened. And she was loving it.

His gaze steady on hers, he turned on his side. She did the same. Stirring lovely shivers in his wake, he skated his palm up over the swell of her hip and then downward along the back of her thigh. Gently, he guided her bare leg up to wrap around him.

He entered her slowly, staring right in her eyes.

Neither of them said a word. They didn't need to. It was so good between them, so natural and right. Her body shimmered with arousal as they moved together. She felt the pleasure rising, a giant wave in a great blue ocean, rearing up high as it raced for the shore.

When she reached the crest, she cried out. Lost in the wonder of that moment, she held Finn tight and whispered his name as she came.

Finn never wanted to leave.

Their Sunday morning was perfect. After a couple of unforgettable hours in bed, they moved on to her kitchen, where she poured him coffee and then cooked eggs over easy with pancakes, link sausages and blackberries she'd picked herself. He ate everything on his plate and then said yes to more.

Back in her bed, they took up where they'd left off.

Her mouth tasted of maple syrup and berries. He couldn't get enough.

His phone started ringing around one o'clock. He sent the first few calls to voicemail. But there were more—texts, too. He had appointments and he was stalling, because he wanted to cancel everything and spend the rest of the day with Kenzie. Sunday night, too, if she would have him.

But she figured out his game. "You're supposed to be working this afternoon, aren't you?"

"Don't remind me," he grumbled. "I'm always working. It never ends."

His sulky expression made her laugh. "Oh, Finn. I don't *have* to remind you. Your phone is already doing that."

As if on cue, his cell buzzed again. "Whoever invented the cell phone should be benched for the season."

She snuggled in close and kissed him, a kiss that started out short and sweet but quickly turned torrid. "One more time," she whispered. He pulled her closer still.

If the phone buzzed or chirped again in the next fifteen minutes, he didn't hear it.

A little while later, she kissed his square jaw and asked, "Coffee to go?"

He buried his lips in her tangled hair. "You really are trying to get rid of me, aren't you?"

"Well, I do have a bunch of random stuff to get done, but if you're really going to blow off your clients, I've got no problem putting off cleaning the bathrooms until some other day—especially not if you do that thing with your tongue again."

He nuzzled her hair some more and stroked his fingers up and down the satiny skin of her forearm. "Which one?"

They laughed together.

And then, he admitted glumly, "I do have to go."

Ten minutes later, Kenzie stood on her porch waving as he drove away.

Back inside, her house was too quiet. She wished that Finn could have stayed. She had such a good time with him. They had fun and there was honesty. They understood each other. Sometimes, when she looked at him, she wished—

Never mind what she wished. This lovely magic between them wasn't going to last and they both knew it. For now, they could be together, enjoy each other, make the most of each day. She just needed to keep herself in check, not let herself get too attached.

She had her home, her community, work she loved and a baby on the way.

Her life was already complete. She didn't need a man to make it so.

Monday was the first day of school.

Kenzie spent that morning dispensing medications, patching up minor injuries and deciding when a student was in bad enough shape to be sent home. By noon, she'd been vomited on by a freshman. And then, Jimmy Trout, a sophomore, came in with a bad nosebleed that he insisted, "Just started out of dowhere, Durse Osborde."

Once she'd stopped the bleeding, she pointed out that he had a cut on his cheekbone and bruises on his knuckles consistent with a fistfight. Jimmy slumped in his chair and muttered that he didn't want to talk about it. She let him sulk right there in her office until the assistant principal could take over.

Kenzie had lunch in the teacher's lounge with Lauren Dalton and Sandy Rice. Sandy taught English and critical thinking. Lauren joked that the students in her earth science class were more interested in throwing spitballs and making googly eyes at each other than in exploring the major cycles that affect every aspect of life.

"Hey, it's high school," said Kenzie. "You know what that means."

Sandy nodded. "Learning, sadly, takes a back seat to picking fights and first love."

"So true," said Lauren.

Now, both Sandy and Lauren were watching Kenzie. Like just about everyone who had grown up there in town, her friends knew that she and Finn had been inseparable all through high school.

Kenzie glanced from Lauren to Sandy and back to Lauren again. She liked and trusted both women. And there was nobody else sitting nearby at the moment. Whatever she said could be kept between the three of them.

However, maybe she was misreading them, thinking they were wondering about her and Finn because the man was constantly on her mind. Maybe neither of her friends had a clue of what was going on between her and Coach Monahan…and she ought to just leave it at that.

The silence at the table stretched out. Sandy and Lauren seemed to be waiting for her to speak. "What?" she demanded.

"Well…" Sandy took a slow sip of her iced tea.

Lauren broke first. She nudged her lunch tray to the side and leaned in. "It was so great seeing you with Finn Monahan at his speech at the Dinosaur Center. You two look good together."

"We're just friends," she said, outright lying. Then again, it wasn't really a lie. They *were* friends—but not *just* friends.

Lauren's eyes were full of understanding. "Hey. It's okay if you don't want to talk about it."

On Kenzie's other side, Sandy lightly squeezed her shoulder. "We care about you, that's all. And we're here. If you need us."

Kenzie blinked away the sudden moisture in her eyes. "Thanks. I mean that. And well, it's just…really hard to trust a guy after a rough divorce." She should stop there. But she didn't. "Plus, Finn and I have some rocky history together, too. Our breakup was a long time ago—but let me tell you, it was brutal."

Her friends were nodding. They were both a little younger than Kenzie and Finn. But it was Tenacity. They must have heard the stories.

Lauren said, "Yeah. You two were legendary. And then he went off to the University of Michigan and you went to Montana State. You came back, but his family moved away and that was that. Eventually, we all knew that it must be over between you two."

"It ended that summer right after graduation," she said. "We only just reconnected recently. We're friends, Finn and me. I think he's great. And, yes, we are spending some time together. But that's all it is, a temporary thing."

"You're saying you can't trust him because he broke your heart all those years ago?" asked Sandy.

"I just don't want to go there. But I don't blame Finn for what went wrong all those years ago. However, between that old heartbreak and the disaster that was my marriage to Tate… I'm kind of done with falling in love. So if you're thinking that Finn and I are getting serious, don't. We're just having fun together, that's all."

"Hey, now…" Sandy looked crestfallen. "Never say never."

Kenzie didn't argue with her. Sandy was still in her twenties, still looking forward to falling madly in love with the perfect man and making a good life with him. Lauren, on the other hand, had been burned by love, too. Like Kenzie, she had the divorce papers to prove it.

"I have to tell you," Lauren said, "I watched you and Finn when we were all hanging out at the Dinosaur Center. You two really do seem to have a connection, like you know each other so well. It's hard to explain. He reached for your hand once when we were all sitting together at the picnic table. You took it and you glanced at him. You smiled at each other, one of those secret smiles, just between the two of you, like you were having a whole conversation that no one else could hear."

Kenzie scoffed. "That never happened."

Lauren threw up both hands. "Fine. Don't believe me. But I know what I saw. It's like the two of you understand each other on a cellular level."

"Science?" Kenzie rolled her eyes. "You're bringing science into this discussion? Lauren, we're talking about men and how some of us aren't sure what they're good for—at least, not anymore."

"Ahem..." Sandy snickered and raised her hand. "I know exactly what they're good for."

"Well, then, share," demanded Kenzie, feeling grateful to be let off the hot seat at least for the moment.

"Love and romance!" declared Sandy triumphantly. "And that upper-body strength does come in handy now and then."

Lauren eyed their colleague with skepticism. "Okay, yes, I did pick up on the vibe between Kenzie and Finn. But Sandy, when it comes to men in general, not all of them are there for the long haul."

"Maybe not." Sandy seemed thoughtful. "But the right man can also be a girl's best friend."

"So can another woman," Kenzie reminded her. "And dogs. Dogs make really great best friends. Personally, I'm thinking of getting a cat. They're soft and cuddly, and they never cheat on you."

"You are so cynical." Sandy sipped her iced coffee. "And nothing against dogs and cats—I have one of each, as you know—but they do have fleas. And sharp teeth. And claws. And what about the barking and the meowing in the middle of the night? Every creature on Earth has flaws. We women have them, too."

Lauren faked a look of total shock. "Women have flaws? How dare you even suggest such a thing?"

Sandy played along. "I know, I know. I've gone too far. Down with the patriarchy! Women rule!"

They all three laughed at that. Across the room, two of their male colleagues eyed them warily.

With a sheepish grin, Lauren whispered out of the side of her mouth, "I guess we'd better keep it down."

"You think?" Kenzie chuckled. And then, she asked,

"Lauren, be straight with me now. Do you honestly believe you'll ever get married again?"

Her friend didn't answer for several seconds. Finally, Lauren sighed. "It's doubtful. But if I ever do say yes again, the fella will have to be something really special."

"'Really special.'" Kenzie groaned. "What does that even mean?"

Sandy raised her hand again. "You need a definition? Leave it to the English teacher. Ahem. Special. It means better, greater, or otherwise different from what is usual. As for *really*, think of it as meaning 'in actual fact,' as opposed to what is said or imagined to be true or possible. Therefore 'really special' means the guy would have to, in actual fact, be better, greater or—"

"Thank you, Ms. Rice," said Lauren with a saccharine smile.

"You're welcome." Sandy gave Lauren gracious little nod.

Kenzie said nothing. She was thinking about Finn.

And Finn was thinking of Kenzie—constantly, as a matter of fact.

That afternoon when he spotted her by the bleachers at practice, he turned the practice over to Barrett and jogged to her side.

"Nurse Osborne," he said. "How're you doing?"

"Real good, Coach," she replied. The wind caught a lock of her shining hair and pulled it free of her topknot. He had to fist his hand at his side to keep from reaching out to smooth it back behind the shell of her ear.

He just wanted to touch her, to pull her against him, cradle her close and kiss the top of her golden head.

But he couldn't do that right there on the football field during practice. And tonight was no good. He had to show a couple of ranch properties right after practice. He should be finished by seven, with any luck. However, if he had to write an offer, it could go on until nine. Even ten.

So not tonight. Or tomorrow. He had to work tomorrow night, too.

"How about dinner Wednesday night?" he asked. "Whatever you're in the mood for. Castillo's? Satterfield's? We could hang out at the Tenacity Social Club if that works for you."

She looked hesitant. He knew she was about to turn him down.

But then she asked, "Do you like cats?"

He had no idea where that question had come from. On second thought, though, it was a hell of a lot better than "no, I won't go out to dinner with you."

"Yeah. Cats are great. They're soft. Furry. The nice ones are affectionate."

"What about dogs?"

"Dogs are also a *yes*. But they're more work than a cat."

"I totally agree with you," she said. "A cat would be better..."

He peered at her more closely. "Are you messing with me?"

She smoothed her hand over her belly, gently, as though to reassure the sleeping baby within. "Maybe. A little." She was trying not to laugh. He could see that now. "But I really am considering getting a pet."

"Then you should get one."

"We'll see..."

The team was waiting on him. "Dinner," he said firmly. "You and me. Wednesday after practice. Say yes."

She frowned as though trying to think of a way to let him down easy. He braced for rejection. But then, she said, "Tell you what. Come to my place. I'll have something ready in the slow cooker."

The relief was unbelievably sweet. Not only would he get an evening with her, but it would also be at her house, in private. Just the two of them. He couldn't suppress a giant, happy smile. "Yes! I'll bring dessert. Something chocolate?"

"How about that crème brûlée from Satterfield's?"

"Great idea. I'll bring that."

"Yum," she replied.

For the next several seconds, they just stood there staring at each other while he thought about holding her, about kissing her.

And kissing her some more...

Finally, she said, "I think Barrett's calling you."

He glanced back at the field. Sure enough, Barrett was waving him over. He waved back and turned to Kenzie again. "Wednesday night."

"I am looking forward to it." She said it softly, for his ears alone.

He jogged back to join the team. When he got there, he blew his whistle to get everyone's attention and then instructed them to grab their phones from their lockers and meet up in the gym.

Several team parents had recorded Friday night's game and Oscar had spent a busy weekend collecting video from the volunteer parents and sending it on to Finn, Barrett and the squad.

That afternoon, the team and the staff spent an hour and a half going over the footage. Finn focused both on what they'd done right and what needed improvement.

After practice, he worked until ten.

Tuesday, he wrote an offer for a large ranch property east of town. The offer was accepted. He would get a good commission when the sale closed. That pleased him. And looking forward to dinner tomorrow night at Kenzie's house pleased him even more. He went to practice that day with a smile on his face.

And then after practice, he put in some time at his office. He got home at 10:00 p.m. He was barely in the door when his phone rang in his pocket.

It was his dad. Finn seriously considered letting it go to voicemail. But family was family. He called his mother twice a month just to check up on her. And he talked to his brothers often.

If he didn't pick up, his dad would just call again. Eventually, Finn would give in and get back to him.

He took the call. "Hello, Dad. How's it going?"

"Your team lost by ten Friday. You need to do better."

Finn put on a smile even though the old man couldn't see it—because there was no point in being angry that his dad was a jerk. Finn Sr. would never change. "I'm doing fine, Dad," Finn said, purposely answering the question his father hadn't asked. "How about you?"

"Let's talk about the Titans and how well you're doing with them."

"The team is doing just great, Dad, thanks."

Finn Sr. made a grumbling sound. "On a happier note,

you not only made *The Bronco Bulletin*, but you also got a mention in the *News-Argus* and *The Bozeman Daily Chronicle*. People are watching you and that is a very good sign."

Finn rubbed his temples. A headache was forming. "Dad—"

"You need a win and you need it this Friday. You need to build that team, and with it, your reputation. Then you land a contract as coach of a decent college team and from there you go on to a better one. Then eventually, if you play your cards right, you're moving up to the NFL, staking your claim as the next big-time NFL coach."

"Dad, I will never be Andy Reid. I don't *want* to be Andy Reid. I sell real estate in my hometown and I help out with the football team and I like it. I like my life. It works for me."

"You're just afraid to reach for the stars."

"I will say it again. I'm coaching the Titans to help out the home team and to build my profile in the community, which helps me sell real estate—also, because I enjoy it. That's it. That's all."

"Don't give me denials. It's not healthy. Get out of your own way..."

There was more. Finn tuned his father out. He let the older man yammer on. When he just couldn't take it anymore, he cut in. "I have to go, Dad."

"Damn it, Finn!"

"My love to Mom. Goodbye."

His father was still berating him as Finn ended the call.

Chapter Seven

Wednesday evening, Kenzie went home as soon as practice was over. Finn kept the team a little longer. He called a huddle to discuss how the practice had gone and to offer tips and encouragement.

It was almost seven when he got to Kenzie's house. She greeted him at the door in one of those flowy skirts of hers and a loose, filmy top.

"You look beautiful," he said. Because she did.

"Thank you." Her cheeks had turned temptingly pink. She glanced down at the to-go bag in his hand. "Is that…?"

"Satterfield's crème brûlée." He handed her the bag. "Two servings in foil ramekins. Instructions for putting them under the broiler to caramelize the topping are in there, too."

She opened the bag and peeked in. "Yum. Even cold, it smells like heaven." She moved back. "Come in, come in…"

"This is really good," Finn announced twenty minutes later as he forked up another bite of Kenzie's slow-cooker spiced turkey and couscous. He chewed slowly, savoring the combination of flavors.

"It's easy and healthy," Kenzie replied. She smiled… and then she frowned. "And I know what you're doing."

"Enjoying this delicious dinner, you mean?" A few minutes ago, he'd made the mistake of mentioning his recent conversation with his dad. Now, he just wanted to leave the unpleasant subject behind. So he ate another bite of couscous. It tasted like apricots and oranges, onion and cinnamon. Cilantro, too.

"Please," Kenzie said. "You're changing the subject. Don't."

"Let's forget about my father—at least until dinner," he suggested. "Talking about him interferes with my appreciation of this excellent meal."

"Eat more slowly. You'll be fine."

He made a face and she made one right back at him. Then he said, "I shouldn't have brought him up."

"Yes, you should. It's good to talk about him with someone who cares for you."

Finn loved the sound of that. "So you care about me, huh?"

Now, she looked simultaneously adorable and annoyed. "Of course, I care about you."

"I'm glad. Because I care about you, too."

"And I'm glad, as well," she said primly. "Now, about your dad…"

He was thinking he'd like to have dinner with her every night. Having dinner with Kenzie seemed to him the perfect way to end the day.

If they were a couple for real, they would tidy up the kitchen together, maybe watch a show. They might discuss whatever family plans they had in the works. And they would hang out with the baby, of course—that is, once the baby was born.

And later, when the baby was sound asleep in her crib, they would go to bed. Together. Some nights they would make slow, perfect love.

And some nights they would simply hold each other. On those nights, they would talk about how their separate days had gone, maybe share their dreams and hopes for their future and the future of their family. Eventually, they would drop off to sleep in each other's arms…

"Finn."

He sat up straighter. "Huh?"

"We were talking about your dad."

"Right…" Why, why, why had he said a word about his dad? And why wouldn't she just let it go?

She stared at him across the table, waiting.

Reluctantly he volunteered, "My dad's… Well, you know how he is. He lives in a world where everything is the way he wants it to be. In that world, his sons have to strive for what he considers success. That I left professional football behind is completely unacceptable to him. He's convinced that I must be disappointed in myself and now he's convinced himself that I moved back to Tenacity as the first step in a supposed plan to become a coach in the NFL."

Her eyes got wide. "Wow."

"Yeah. Unbelievable, huh? Let me just make this clear. I am not disappointed in myself or my life. Not in the least. I like my life now."

"Hmm." She forked up a bite of tossed salad and chewed it thoughtfully.

He looked at her warily. "What are you thinking?"

She sipped from her tall glass of ice water. As she set her glass down, she said, "Well, Finn. Your father's assumption that you're planning to get back into professional football isn't all that far-fetched. You *were* a star NFL quarterback."

"Yeah, for about ten minutes."

"Don't minimize your accomplishments. You won MVP two years running and that second year, you went all the way to the championship."

"And in the third game of my third season, I tore my ACL. It was downhill from there."

"Not the point. You're a golden boy. And your injured knee won't stand in the way of a possible coaching career."

"I didn't say it would. I just said that I only had a couple of great years in the NFL. As for being a golden boy, that ship has sailed. I barely got started before I was finished."

"But your start was spectacular. People know your name. And you know the game. Your father's idea of your future is within the realm of possibility if that's what you want."

"I don't."

She made a low, puzzled sound. "You don't?"

"No, I don't want to coach professional football. I honestly don't. I like my life the way it is right now. I like living here in my hometown. I like *being* here as Tenacity comes into its own again. I like helping out any way I can. And I like making money selling houses to folks who will put down roots here and help make our town grow, make Tenacity the kind of place people want to live and raise their families.

"Yes, I'm having a great time working with the Titans. But that doesn't mean I have any desire to be a coach in the NFL."

Kenzie was staring at him so intently. A single tear slid down her soft cheek.

"Kenz?" He shoved back his chair and stood. "What is it? Are you okay?"

She sniffled, waved a hand at him and commanded, "Sit back down. I'm *fine*."

Slowly, he sank to his chair. "But you're crying…"

"It's nothing." Another tear fell. She swiped it away. "Just hormones." He didn't believe her. And that must have shown on his face, because she added with a groan, "If you must know, it's…well, what you just said was beautiful, that's all."

Now, he had no idea what to say next. "Yeah, well. It's only the truth."

"I'm just going to get up and get a tissue, okay? I'll be right back." She headed for the short hall to her room. When she returned, he kept his mouth shut—except to put food in it—for the next several minutes. Eventually, he said, "I've been thinking about that cat you said you wanted."

She looked adorably flummoxed. "What cat?"

"The other day at practice, remember? You said you were considering getting a cat…or a dog."

"Oh, that. I was just thinking out loud."

"So you *don't* want a pet?"

"I'm not sure." She gestured at her baby bump. "As you might have noticed, I have lot going on. But I do miss having pets."

"I thought so. And I did some research. I suggest a

cat. They don't take as much training and they do better when left on their own than a dog does." She was looking at him strangely. He asked, "What's wrong?"

"Nothing. Just thinking about you, thinking how you and your brothers had no pets growing up…"

"You're right, we never had so much as a goldfish."

"If I remember correctly, that was your dad's doing."

"Yeah. He always said animals were messy and he didn't see the point. And then later, when I was playing pro ball, I never felt all that settled, never felt I had time for a pet."

"That is just sad."

He shrugged. "It is what it is."

She shook her head. "Your dad. What a guy."

"Can we not get side-tracked into talking about my dad?"

She grinned then. "Fair enough. Forget your dad."

"Happy to—and listen, if I'm way off-base and you don't even want a cat, you should just say so now."

She pushed her empty plate to the side, braced her elbow on the table and rested her chin on the heel of her palm. "I haven't had a cat in years. My ex was like your dad. Not a pet person."

"So you *are* interested in adopting a cat?"

"You know what? Yeah. I am. Tell me about this research that you did."

"Sure. You should get two cats. They will be happier and they'll keep each other company when you're at school or whatever. Shelter cats are great unless you want some specific breed."

"Not really. Just, you know, a *nice* cat—or I guess, two nice cats."

"Okay. A cat without papers costs anywhere from nothing to over two hundred bucks depending on the source. Then there are vet bills, neutering and spaying, shots, all that. There are also cat supplies and food. All that can get expensive."

"Honestly, I can swing it financially. We always had cats and a dog when I was growing up. There's something so reassuring about having pets around. When they bond with you, they teach you the meaning of devotion. I want that for my little girl."

"So, then if you're going to do this, they should be indoor cats. Cats that don't eat prey or raw meat."

"Why?"

"To protect against toxoplasmosis, a parasitic infection that can cause birth defects or miscarriage."

"Yikes!" She was wide-eyed. "You really did look into this."

"Might as well be prepared, right?"

"Definitely, and I think I read about toxoplasmosis somewhere. Pregnant women get infected from cleaning the litter box."

"But you won't have a problem if you keep your cats indoors. And you can have them tested—and treated, if necessary—before you bring them home. And wear nitrile gloves when you clean the litter box to be extra safe." He was watching her face. Was she skeptical? "You don't seem all that sure about this."

"I'm thinking it sounds like a lot. And I'm gone all day five days a week. It seems wrong to bring two cats home and then start out by leaving them alone all day."

"Yeah, I thought about that and I think I have a solution for you."

"You really want me to have a cat, don't you?"

"Only if *you* really want one."

She was looking at him strangely. Finally, she said, "I kind of can't believe you've been figuring out how a divorced pregnant woman with a full-time job might be able to adopt a cat…or two."

"Hey. What are friends for?"

She laughed then. He'd always loved her laugh. It was husky and low. "Before we go any further on this subject, how about dessert?" she asked.

Together, they cleared the table. She got the coffee going and turned on the broiler to finish off the crème brûlée. In no time, they were sipping coffee and enjoying their dessert, which wasn't quite as pretty as the one they'd been served at Satterfield's, but still really good.

She broke the silence. "Now, about the cats…"

"I knew it. You really do miss having pets."

"Yes. Cats and dogs are loving and loyal and they never cheat on you."

He wanted to grab her and hold her right then. But he stayed in his seat. "I hear you. Let's figure out a way that you can have what you want."

"Oh, Finn. As I said before, I can't see how it's doable. I just wouldn't be around enough, especially at first while they're getting used to living here."

"So how about if I come by and check on them while you're at work?"

She was already shaking her head. "No. Finn, that's not—"

"Just hear me out."

"But it's not fair to you," she insisted. He kept his

mouth shut and stared at her steadily until she put up both hands. “Fine. Go ahead.”

“Okay, so it’s like this. Monday through Friday, I have free time during the day because most of my clients are at work themselves. That means for the first few weeks after you adopt, I can drop by when I have an hour or two to spare. While I’m here I’ll deal with the litter box and hang out with the cats, help them to get adjusted to their new home.”

“Finn, really. That’s too much to ask.”

“No, it’s not. Besides, you’re not asking. I’m volunteering.”

“But why?”

“Because I can. Because when I was growing up, I never had pets and I always wanted one. Because there are cats that need homes. Because friends help friends.” Also, he was coming to accept the fact that he would do just about anything for the woman across the table from him.

No way would he admit that now, though. She had her rules when it came to this thing between them. He had to be careful not to overstep. Anything that sounded too much like *Kenzie, I’m falling in love with you all over again* could have her suddenly deciding they were spending too much time together.

She was silent. He had no idea what she might be thinking.

Finally, she asked, “You’re sure about this?”

“I wouldn’t have offered if I wasn’t.”

“Well, okay then. Thank you. Thank you so much. I’m going to start asking around town, see if anyone wants to give a pair of littermates away to a good home.

And if that doesn't work out, there's an animal sanctuary in Bronco." The larger town was a ninety-minute drive west of Tenacity. "I'll check there if I don't have any luck locally."

He offered, "Let me know how I can help."

She gave him that look from under her lashes. "You've already volunteered to entertain my furry friends and clean their litter box. I figure the least I can do is find them and bring them home in the first place."

"Kenz."

"Yeah?"

He considered how much to say, and admitted, "I like hanging out with you. Whatever you need, I want to help make it happen. Is it okay with you if I check around, too?"

"You sure?"

"Positive."

After another thoughtful silence, she gave him permission. "Yes, then. Check around."

They shared a long look. He thought how he could get lost in those eyes of hers. And that mouth…

Too tempting by far.

His chair scraped the floor as he pushed it back. Swiftly, he circled the table to stand at her side.

She looked up at him and slowly smiled. "Finn Monahan, what *are* you thinking?"

He offered his hand. She took it. He pulled her to her feet. She came into his arms with a soft little sigh. After a long, tender kiss, she took his hand and led him to her room.

Finn didn't get home until after midnight. But the next day he had nothing to take care of workwise until a showing at noon. He was up at nine and fixing himself some breakfast when his housekeeper, Marlene, appeared.

As usual, he was thinking of Kenzie as he microwaved oatmeal. The microwave beeped. He pulled open the door and took out the bowl. "Hey, Marlene, you wouldn't happen to know anyone in town with kittens or grown cats to give away to a good home, would you?"

Marlene, who was six feet tall, rail-slim and wore her long black hair in a fat topknot, scowled at him disapprovingly. "What do you need with a cat? You're hardly ever home. Even a cat would get lonely around here."

"It's for someone else. And I need more than one." He went on to explain what he was looking for.

Marlene narrowed her eyes. "These cats for your girlfriend?"

He played it cool. "Who said I have a girlfriend, Marlene?"

"Honey, you're not in the big city anymore. Everybody in town knows that you and Nurse Osborne have a little thing going on—not that it's anybody's business but yours." Marlene winked. "I think it's great. And I might be able to help you with the cat situation. I'll ask around."

"Thank you."

"For you, anything." She patted his shoulder and got to work with the vacuum cleaner.

That afternoon, as he was wrapping up some loose ends in his office at Big Sky Properties before heading to the high school for practice, Marlene called. He picked up on the first ring.

"Hello, Marlene. Do you have good news for me?"

She did. Marlene gave him the phone number of her cousin, Ardella, who had six kittens old enough to be adopted. "She's giving them away to good homes," Marlene said. "But take my word for it. Ardella never missed a chance to make a buck. Don't let her talk you into paying for those kittens."

"But if she—"

"Okay, okay. I get it. It's not like you're hurting for cash. And if you're willing to pay a little, okay. But you gotta draw the line with Ardella or she'll be charging you pet-store prices. And then you'll still have to take them to the vet for shots and all that."

"I will be firm," he promised his housekeeper.

"Humph," Marlene replied. "You haven't met Ardella yet." She rattled off her cousin's number.

He started to call Ardella but then decided he'd better run it by Kenzie first.

She answered his call on the first ring. "Talk fast. It's a zoo around here. Someone else could come in with a nosebleed or a bad case of the stomach flu any minute now. Not that either of those events are out of the ordinary. It's a rare day when I don't end up using a disinfectant wipe to clean blood and or vomit from my scrubs."

He asked carefully, "So then, I shouldn't call you at work?"

"Of course, you should. Just be prepared to listen to me go on about stuff you have no desire to hear."

"Got it."

"Now, what can I do for you, Finn?"

He gave her the news, along with Ardella's number.

She laughed. "Thank you!" He could hear the happy smile in her voice. "I'll call her before practice. You are the best."

He hung up feeling great. Kenzie wanted cats and he'd gotten right on that for her.

He caught up with her at practice.

When he asked if she'd had time to contact Ardella, she nodded. "I'm going over there after we're done here. I've called the vet in town. The receptionist said I can bring the kittens in today for shots and testing."

"But—"

"I know, I know." She was beaming from ear to ear. "I haven't even seen them yet. But they're kittens, Finn. What's not to love?"

"I'm sure they're adorable. Just let me go with you to Ardella's house."

"You don't have to do that."

"Oh, yes, I do. I'm the one who set you up with Ardella."

She looked at him for an uncomfortable count of five. "And…"

"My housekeeper gave me Ardella's number. The kittens are supposed to be for free, but I've been warned that Ardella will try to get money for them. My housekeeper says it's important to draw the line with Ardella."

Now, Kenzie was giving him a look of great patience. "I think I can handle the situation myself, Finn."

"I'm sure you can. But come on. Let me go with you."

"Because you want to or because you think I'm somehow going to get taken advantage of?"

"Because I want to. Plus, I'm a crackerjack negotiator. And I admit, I'm curious about Ardella."

"Well, okay then." She grinned wide. "Today's your lucky day."

"Great!" he said. "And tomorrow's game day. The guys need to be fresh and alert, so today's practice will be short. That means we'll be out of here by five, five thirty at the latest."

"That'll work. The vet closes at six but the receptionist said she'd wait around for me."

He wanted to grab her and claim those sweet lips of hers. Unfortunately, sharing torrid kisses with Nurse Osborne right there on the football field would in no way be considered appropriate behavior.

With a nod, he turned and headed back to join the team.

Ardella was a real pistol.

Even taller than her cousin Marlene, Ardella wore her platinum-blond hair in a beehive worthy of Amy Winehouse complete with a ponytail that she combed forward over one shoulder. That ponytail fell almost to her waist. She introduced herself and her husband, Earl, said they were new to Tenacity. Retirees, they'd bought their house for practically nothing two years before.

"But things are looking good around here now," Ardella declared. "Right, Earl?"

"Right, Sugar Bear," Earl replied. He sat in a giant recliner with two cats in his lap watching infomercials on the big screen mounted over the fireplace.

Ardella had at least five grown cats—the two on Earl's lap and three more that Finn spotted lurking under a table and peeking out from behind a sideboard. As for the kittens, they were all shorthairs in a variety of colors. They zipped around the living area, batting at shadows, knocking cat toys under tables and wrestling with each other.

Kenzie had a hard time choosing. Finn got a kick out of watching her cuddle each kitten, declare it the one… and then say the same thing about the next one she got her hands on. Finally, she settled on one of the two black cats and a gray tabby, both male.

"I've got an extra carrier I can sell you," said Ardella. "Those kittens can share it for now. I also have a few cat toys you can buy off me. And a cute little cat bed. As for those kittens, fifty bucks each."

Finn spoke up then. "Now, just wait a—"

Kenzie stopped him with a look. Then she smiled sweetly at Ardella. "Twenty each for these sweet babies of yours."

Finn held his breath as the two women stared at each other, eye to eye and will to will.

Eventually, Ardella cackled out a laugh. "I'm a sucker for a real cat lover." She flicked that long ponytail back over her shoulder. "Fine. Twenty each. And twenty for the cat carrier. Ten for the bed. The toys are five each."

Kenzie took everything Ardella had offered. The two women hugged each other at the door.

"Bye, Earl!" Kenzie gave him a wave.

"You take care now!" Earl called back from the comfort of his recliner.

From Ardella's house, they drove straight to the veterinary clinic on the eastern edge of town. Hoof and Paw Animal Care was run by two veterinarians. A married couple, the husband treated large animals and the wife was a small-animal vet.

By the time Finn and Kenzie got there, the office was closed for the day, but the receptionist, Anna, had stuck around as promised. Anna checked in the kittens and reassured Kenzie that they would be well looked after during their stay.

"I will call you as soon as the test results come in," Anna promised. "That should be early next week. You should be able to take them home that day, unless they test positive. Then they'll be staying with us a little longer for treatment."

Outside, a warm wind was blowing and the sun had begun sinking toward the horizon. Finn caught Kenzie's hand when they reached her car.

She gave his fingers a squeeze and then moved in close enough to lean her head on his shoulder with a sigh.

He asked, "What's wrong?"

She made a soft sound low in her throat. "They've been mine for less than an hour and yet I miss them already."

He pulled her close and stroked a hand down her shining hair. "You'll have them back before you know it."

"You're right." She smiled up at him. "I'll get online tomorrow and order food, a litter box and all the cat gear I can think of."

"Don't forget to start thinking of names for them."

"I've already named them."

"Tell me," he whispered in her ear.

"The black one is Tom and the tabby is Ed."

Finn approved. "Solid, serviceable names."

"That's right. They're regular guys. They like to bat their toys around and fake-fight with each other. If they were human, they would grow up to enjoy a beer at the Grizzly Bar." She slanted him a sideways look. "I've got leftovers in the fridge."

"Is that an invitation?"

She slid a soft hand up to wrap around his neck. “Come down here.” He could not obey fast enough. The wind blew around them and he kissed her slow and deep. Somewhere off toward the distant mountains, a hawk cried. When he lifted his head, she added, “Yes, that is an invitation. Follow me home?”

Gently, he guided a windblown lock of pale hair away from her lips. “I would follow you anywhere,” he said, and kissed her again.

Chapter Eight

Finn didn't check his messages until he got back to his place at midnight. There were several from clients and the office, so on Friday, he scrambled to catch up, to see that everyone got what they needed.

But he smiled through it all. Kenzie had found the kittens she'd been longing for and he'd helped make that happen. Then she'd invited him home with her, fed him dinner and taken him to bed.

Life was good and bound to get even better.

Yeah, she claimed she was through with love, that she would be raising her baby on her own. But sometimes, when he held her close and looked in her eyes, he knew that deep down she wanted what he wanted—another chance at the forever they'd lost when they were teenagers.

No, they weren't there yet. But they would get there. He just knew it.

And not only were things going well with Kenzie, but the Titans were really stepping up, showing him both grit and dedication. Those boys got better every day. They loved the game and they gave it their all.

Friday afternoon, the team radiated excitement and energy as they boarded the school bus for Big Dusty,

Montana. When the bus pulled in at Big Dusty High, home of the Eagles, Kenzie and the team moms and dads were already there.

At kickoff, the bleachers were packed on both sides. T-Grizz and the cheer squad got the Tenacity fans going as Dusty the Eagle and the Big Dusty cheerleaders got their team fired up.

The game went into overtime. But the Titans triumphed 14–7. At the team meeting in the Eagles' girls' locker room afterward, Finn had nothing but praise for his players. The bus ride back home was a happy one.

At 1:05 a.m. Saturday morning in the Tenacity High parking lot, Finn and Barrett thanked Oscar for the good work and watched him drive off with his dad.

A moment later, Barrett's fiancée, Nina, drove up. She jumped out to give her future husband a steamy congratulatory kiss. Finn laughed and advised the two of them to get a room. Then he stood there in the darkness waving as they drove away, thinking about Kenzie, who was probably home already, tucked into her bed.

He was turning to head for his truck when a familiar Bronco pulled in right beside him. Suddenly the empty parking lot seemed to shimmer with promise.

"Lookin' for a ride, big guy?" Kenzie called out her window.

He stepped right up and leaned in close. "Hey."

They shared a kiss through the open window, one every bit as steamy as the one Barrett had planted on Nina a few minutes before. When Finn started to pull back, she grabbed his shoulder and yanked him close again. What could he do? If Kenzie wanted another kiss, he was so there for that.

Finally, she gave a low laugh against his parted lips. "Follow me home?"

"You're on."

Finn woke to sunlight streaming in Kenzie's bedroom window. She was already awake, and grinning at him.

"What?" he asked. "Something's funny?"

"Nope."

"So, then…?"

"You're just all cute and cuddly when you're sleeping."

He thought that over for a minute. "Cute and cuddly, huh?"

"Don't be offended," she advised. "Manly men can be cute and cuddly, too."

He kissed the tip of her nose. "If you say so."

"I do. How about some breakfast?"

He pulled her closer and claimed her sweet mouth. She felt just right in his arms, the round fullness of her belly pressed close against him. He could so easily see himself waking up next to her every morning for the rest of his life—not that he would say that out loud to her at this point. She had her rules, after all.

"Breakfast?" she asked again.

"Hmm. I don't know. I think I just want to lie here in this bed with you all day long."

On the nightstand, his phone chose that moment to ping with a text. He ignored it.

Kenzie didn't. "That thing does a lot of pinging."

"Happy to silence it."

She reached up and gently brushed his hair back off his forehead. "Nah. I just mean, you work hard. And I bet you have appointments today."

"Not until this afternoon."

"What about recovery practice."

"It's not till ten. We have plenty of time."

"Really?"

"Really." He pulled her closer.

She giggled like a little kid. "I can feel exactly how glad you are to see me."

He nuzzled her throat, breathing in her sweet scent. "Let me show you how glad…"

She giggled again. Slowly, he slid hand down between them. Her giggle ended on a sigh.

Monday was Labor Day. That meant no school and no practice. Finn took the day off from selling real estate, too.

Too bad reporters never seemed to take a break. More than one of them had found Finn's school email address and used it to reach out for an interview. He debated getting back to them and ended up deciding that a little properly managed PR would be good for Tenacity and for the Titans. He answered those emails and agreed to be interviewed via Zoom.

In total, he took five Zoom calls that day, two with reporters from Montana outlets and three with writers from out of state. They wanted to know all about the former NFL quarterback who just might be leading his home team to a state championship.

Once he'd finished the Zoom interviews, he called Kenzie and talked her into meeting him at the Silver Spur Café.

The cozy Western-style diner served breakfast and

lunch. And as usual, it was packed. They lucked out, though, and got a deuce tucked back in a corner.

Too bad their private nook didn't stop people from dropping by their table to talk football. Or to bring up how great it was to see the two of them together. Nobody added "after all these years," but the look in their eyes said it for them.

"We're just good friends," Kenzie insisted more than once.

Nobody argued the point. But judging by their knowing grins, nobody believed her, either.

Finn certainly didn't. He saw what everyone else saw. The two of them were growing closer. He really did want to take what they had to the next level. It was getting harder for him not to push for more.

Yes, she kept insisting that what they had wasn't serious. But she was wrong.

He knew that they could make it work this time, the two of them…and her baby girl. He wasn't some selfish, confused kid anymore. He knew what he wanted now.

And what he wanted was Kenzie. If she could see her way clear to giving him a second chance, he wouldn't blow it. Not this time.

This time, he would get it right.

Too bad he couldn't quite make himself have that talk with her. He knew damn well that if he tried for everything, he risked losing it all.

Kenzie got the call from Anna at Hoof and Paw on Tuesday morning. Tom and Ed had tested negative for toxoplasmosis. They'd also had their shots. She could bring her kittens home today.

As soon as she hung up with Anna, she called Finn to share the good news.

"That is just great," he said.

"I know, right?"

"So then, what's your plan?"

"Oh, Finn. I am so glad you asked…"

He laughed, a low, rich sound that made her breath catch and a shiver slide over her skin. "I'm listening," he said.

"Well, I don't want to wait until after practice to bring them home. I want to use my lunch break to get them settled in. But then, I'll just have to leave them and get back to work. Any chance you could meet me at my house, maybe stay for a while, keep them company for a bit after I have to go?"

The man didn't even hesitate. "Yeah. No problem. I'll meet you at Hoof and Paw, help out any way you need me there and then I'll follow you home."

It was exactly what she was hoping he might say. But really, she'd been taking total advantage of him lately and she couldn't help but think that she should give the man a break. "Honestly, you could just meet me at my place around noon."

"What time will you be at the vet's to pick them up?"

"Finn." She put on her best no-nonsense voice.

"Kenzie," he replied in a similar tone.

"I get the feeling you're not listening to me."

"Because I'm not. What time will you be at Hoof and Paw?"

She let out a loud sigh. "I give up."

"Finally. What time?"

* * *

When she arrived at the veterinarian's office she found Finn leaning against his fancy crew cab, big arms folded across his broad chest. His Stetson shaded his eyes and he had on his team jacket.

She parked in the empty space beside him. By the time she pulled to a stop, he'd already walked around to the rear of her vehicle. He tapped on the hatch and she popped it. Then he grabbed the cat carrier, shut the liftgate and rounded the back of the Bronco to join her as she got out of the car.

"Ready?" he asked.

"Thanks for this." She leaned up and kissed him. His lips were warm. She smiled into the kiss…and as soon as he lifted his head, she realized she probably shouldn't have done that. "For some reason, I can't quit kissing you. It's getting so bad I'm doing it right out here in broad daylight for anyone driving by to see."

He gave an easy shrug. "It's okay. I like kissing you. Feel free to make a move on me whenever the mood strikes."

"Please. If I keep kissing you in public, nobody will believe me when I tell them that we're just good friends."

"Face it." He was smirking. "The *just-good-friends* ship has sailed. You saw the looks on their faces yesterday at the Silver Spur. They've all decided we've got a thing going on, that we are getting our second chance at true love."

"That doesn't mean we have to encourage them in their delusion," she grumbled.

"On the contrary, Nurse Osborne. I like kissing you and I don't care who's watching or what they think about it, either." Then he bent close and kissed her again.

She probably shouldn't have kissed him back. But, hey. It was a beautiful day and she was bringing her kittens home.

Not to mention the man could kiss. And she loved that he would be there to help Tom and Ed feel more comfortable on their first day at her house.

Inside the vet's office, Kenzie paid the bill. Anna took the carrier and disappeared down the hallway to the left of the front desk. A moment later, a tall woman in green scrubs emerged from the same hallway.

"Hello!" she said, offering her hand to Kenzie and then to Finn. "I'm Dr. Sparling, the veterinarian in charge here at the clinic. It's so good to meet you both. And I'm happy to tell you that your kittens are healthy, fully vaccinated and ready to go home." The vet went on to talk about neutering and when to bring Tom and Ed in for that. Finally, Anna reappeared with the cat carrier.

"Oh, look!" Kenzie teared up. "Here they are…" As if in reply, the kittens launched into a two-part chorus of meows.

At her house, she had everything ready for Ed and Tom. As soon as she let them out the carrier, off they darted to explore their new home. She made Finn a sandwich and then hung around for a half hour or so. She wished she could stay longer. But he was there to keep the kittens company for a while after she left and that made her feel better.

He walked her to the door where she handed him a house key.

"Because you'll need to get in and out now. Thank you, for babysitting my kitties."

"Are you kidding? I should thank you. I'm going to love hanging out with Tom and Ed."

She kissed him then, a long, slow, deep kiss. "You're the best." She beamed up at him.

And then she made herself turn and head for her car.

For the remainder of that week, Finn couldn't walk down the street without everyone he passed stopping to clap him on the back and tell him what a hero he was. He thanked them for their kind words and praised the team—their talent, determination and fighting spirit.

That Friday the Titans played at home. They racked up an impressive win. Final score: 38–9.

The crowd went wild.

Much later, when Finn left the by-then quiet locker room and headed for the parking lot, most of the vehicles had cleared out. But Kenzie's blue Bronco was waiting beside his crew cab.

She stood by her driver's door in her maroon scrubs, that shining hair in a thick braid, her hands in the pockets of a plaid barn coat, watching him as he came toward her. "We've got to stop meeting in parking lots," she teased.

He kept walking until the toes of his boots were six inches from hers. "Hey." He touched her cheek, so smooth and soft. "It's how we roll."

She reached for him. He pulled her close and she wrapped her arms around his neck. "Come to my place," she whispered. "Ed and Tom have been nagging me for a playdate with you."

"I was there just this afternoon. We played catch the feather and bat the jingle ball."

"What can I tell you? You're a popular guy. And not only with Tom and Ed."

"That's what I wanted to hear." He claimed a long, slow kiss.

A little later, at Kenzie's place, she went off to change her clothes. Finn sat on the living-room floor sipping a Bud Light and tormenting the two playful kittens with a string of feathers on a stick.

It wasn't long before Kenzie reappeared in gray joggers and a big pink shirt. "Mind if I join you?"

He patted the floor beside him. "You need help getting down here?"

She put on a playful scowl. "I beg your pardon. I'm pregnant, not incapacitated."

"You are beautiful," he said. "Even when you make silly faces."

Ed chose that moment to leap into his lap, jump at the feather and then dart off through the archway to Kenzie's office with Tom right behind him.

"They do make me laugh," she said.

He set his beer on the coffee table then offered a hand. She took it and he helped her down. Settling in beside him, she managed to sit cross-legged, her baby bump cradled between her thighs.

The kittens came racing back. She rested her head on his shoulder and laughed as they batted at the uncatchable feathers.

Finn thought about how good it was between them, how easy and right. Once again, he considered bringing up the future. He ached to ask her to spend that future with him.

But was it too soon? He didn't want to blow it.

Better to wait a while, he decided. Better to give her more time to see all the ways he would be there for her and for the baby—for Tom and Ed, too.

Eventually, the kittens ran off again, toward the kitchen this time. Finn got up, set the feather toy on the mantel and held down his hand to Kenzie. She took it and he pulled her to her feet. They turned for her bedroom together, his arm around her shoulders, her hand hooked at his waist. He didn't realize that Tom and Ed were right behind them until he and Kenzie entered the bedroom and two small balls of fur zipped around them and launched themselves up onto the bed.

Kenzie laughed. "Okay, you two. You've got your own bed."

Reluctantly, Finn let her go. She scooped up both kittens and carried them from the room. Returning a couple of minutes later, she shut the door behind her.

"Do they sleep with you?" he asked, pulling her close again, getting hold of that long braid, giving it a light tug.

"Yep. Most of the time. But not right now."

"Will they be lonely?" After sliding the elastic band off the tail of that braid, he snapped it onto his wrist.

She gazed up at him, eyes bright as stars. "Nope. They have each other. They like sleeping in my bed, but they're just fine on their own, too."

He smoothed her unbound hair back over her shoulder. It fell almost to her waist. He longed to say what was in his heart. But no. Not yet.

Instead, he whispered, "You are so beautiful," and lowered his mouth to hers.

Kenzie woke Saturday morning to a chorus of meows from the other side of her bedroom door. Finn was sound asleep next to her. Carefully, trying not to wake him, she pushed back the covers, slid her feet to the floor and put on her robe.

The meows got more insistent as she padded to the door and pulled it open a crack. That was all it took. Ed slithered in first with Tom right behind him.

"Shh," she said, as if they would care, let alone listen.

They raced to the bed and climbed it in an instant, landing on the side where she'd slept. Stopping simultaneously, they stared at the other person in her bed.

They knew Finn. After all, he provided their day care. For a second or two, they seemed to study the sleeping man. Then both kittens started purring. They moved in close to Finn. Ed batted Finn's cheek gently with a tiny paw. Tom climbed right on top of him and sat down. Kenzie stifled a laugh as Finn opened his eyes to find Tom perched on his chest.

"Mornin' ,Tomás." Finn scooped up the little guy and set him down on the mattress. Then he rolled to his side and petted Ed. "How you doin', Eduardo?"

Still in her robe, Kenzie lifted the covers and slid back into the bed. Tom's purr got louder as she stroked a hand from his head to the tip of his shiny black tail. "Sorry they woke you."

Finn gave her a lazy grin. "Don't be sorry. I'm not. They're so damn cute."

For a while, they hung out in bed with the kittens, who wrestled with their hands and chewed on their fingers. Kenzie was scratching Ed behind the ears and he was purring away when she glanced up and caught Finn watching her.

"What?"

"Nothing. Just…it's so good, being here with you."

His words pleased her.

Maybe too much.

Was she getting in too deep with him? Probably.

But he was right. It *was* good—better even than back in high school, when she'd loved him wildly, needed him desperately. She might be seriously pregnant with occasional heartburn and ankles that now had a tendency to swell. Didn't matter.

Finn still had that uncanny ability to look in her eyes and make her feel like the most beautiful woman on earth. Sometimes, when he kissed her, when he put his big hands on her and whispered her name, her poor heart felt full to bursting. With Finn now, it was the same as all those years ago.

Only better. Deeper. More grounded somehow.

She cared about him and she wanted him constantly. They truly were friends. As for falling in love with him all over again…

No. That wasn't going to happen. Her heart just wasn't up for that.

He was watching her. "What?" he asked as Tom yawned and stretched between them. The little black cat purred even louder as Ed bent his gray-striped head and started grooming Tom's ear.

"Oh, nothing," she lied. "How 'bout some breakfast?"

"I thought you'd never ask."

Finn had just finished his scrambled eggs when his phone rang.

Kenzie met his eyes across the table. "Not even going to check and see who it is?"

"It's too early for phone calls." And no way he wanted

to be interrupted while he was with her. "I'll check my voicemail later."

He said yes to more coffee and fantasized about dragging her back to bed.

But there was recovery practice to deal with. Too soon, he was on his way to his place, where he jumped in the shower before heading to the high school.

After practice, he cleaned up and hosted an open house right there in town. He had a steady stream of visitors. Back at the office later, he checked messages and discovered that the call earlier that morning had been from his dad. He actually considered just ignoring his father's voicemail. Because no message from Finn Sr. ever made Finn's day brighter.

But just maybe his dad was calling with family news. Maybe one of his brothers had gotten engaged. Or what if someone was seriously ill or had been in an accident?

He played back the message.

"Finn. Congratulations on your recent wins—two of them, I hear. And the win last night… Wow, thirty-eight to nine. Impressive. Plus, I've read those interviews you gave last week. Son, you can't fool me. I know what you're doing. Don't give me that crap about how you're just pitching in, helping out the home team. Don't try to tell me you plan to sell run-down ranchettes out there on the prairie for the rest of your life. You're making a move. You can't fool your old man. Call me back. We'll talk strategy."

Finn almost threw his phone at the far wall.

His dad did that to him sometimes. Made him want to break things, made him want to toss back his head and scream at the ceiling like a toddler throwing a tantrum.

Finn Sr. made decisions about how things should be and then obstinately expected everyone to go along, to do whatever he wanted them to do. To change their lives to suit his own personal ideas about who mattered and what counted.

Finn should probably just call him back and tell him to get the hell over himself, maybe even try to make him see how far off-base he was. But hadn't he done exactly that the last time the old man called?

He just didn't feel like trying again right now.

Finn deleted the message and got on with his day.

Kenzie made it through Saturday night and Sunday morning without giving in to her ridiculous eagerness to reach out to Finn, to ask him if maybe he had a little free time that afternoon. They could hang out with the kittens. Take a walk around town or sit out on the back deck at his place watching the prairie grass rustle in the wind, maybe spot a hawk or an eagle soaring high in the clear blue sky.

Somehow, she kept herself from contacting him. Yes, they were friends—good friends, with benefits. But they both needed their space, after all. They both needed to remember that they had separate lives, and alone time was a good thing.

On Monday, Finn was already on the field when she arrived for practice. Her silly heart actually skipped a beat when he spotted her and came jogging over.

"Good weekend?" he asked.

"It was thrilling. I cleaned out the refrigerator and mopped the kitchen floor."

He stepped a little closer. "Tom and Ed were glad to see me today when I dropped in at noon."

She truly did love that he checked in on the kittens when she couldn't be there. "Thank you."

"Hey. It's Tom and Ed. I should thank *you*."

"Right… But you will let me know if stopping in to see them gets old, right?"

"You bet. But it hasn't happened yet."

For a long, weirdly wonderful moment, they just stood there by the bleachers, grinning at each other.

He broke the smile-fest. "You free tonight? Let's get some dinner. We could go out or—"

"Come to my house," she said, sounding ridiculously eager to he own ears. "I'll, um, fix us something."

He looked at her like she'd offered him the moon, but then he said, "Come to my place instead."

"I really shouldn't."

He knew why without her having to say more. "Tom and Ed will be lonely."

"Yeah. I haven't seen them since I left for work this morning. And they are just babies, you know."

"Yes, I do." His eyes made the kind of promises that had her breath coming faster. "Bring them to my place."

"I would love to, but—"

"Not in the mood to haul all their gear over there with you?" One corner of his mouth had kicked up in a crooked smile.

"Exactly," she said. "It's kind of a lot."

"No problem. Just so happens I bought a litter box and the litter to go with it, food, bowls, a cat bed and some toys I think they might like."

She actually gasped. "You didn't!"

"Oh, yes, I did. What can I say? I've been promising them a playdate at my place."

"Oh, so they understand English now?"

"Of course, they do. They're very bright boys. And now that I've made them a promise, their feelings will be hurt if I don't follow through. It's a trust issue. They count on me to keep my word. If I don't, they'll grow up cynical and unable to form meaningful relationships."

"Oh, Finn..." Too bad grabbing him in a hug would be wildly inappropriate given that they were in plain sight of the entire football team.

He suggested sheepishly, "I was kind of hoping you might pick them up and bring them along with you. I'll get takeout from Satterfield's."

What could she say? He'd won her over completely back at the part where he said he'd bought everything her kittens would need to feel at home at his house. "I can't stay too late."

"I know. School tomorrow. I promise I won't keep you past...?" He waited, letting her fill in the time.

"I really should leave by nine."

"Nine. Got it." He swept off his hat. "That's a yes, then? Dinner at my place, Ed and Tom included."

"That is a yes."

Finn had a plan and his plan worked perfectly.

Later, at his place, they ate fork-tender filets, roasted potatoes and grilled asparagus as Tom and Ed batted a jingle ball around at their feet. They cleaned up after the meal together.

What was it about cleaning up the kitchen after dinner with Kenzie? Finn asked himself. It flat-out made him want to take her to bed.

Then again, it didn't matter what they were doing. He was constantly thinking about getting her out of her clothes.

He kept his hands to himself for as long as he could. Objectively, it wasn't long at all. It only took a few minutes to clear off the table and load the dishwasher.

As he shut the dishwasher door, she was wiping the last counter, the one by the sink. All he had to do was take one step in her direction.

They kissed. A long, slow, sweet, perfect kiss. Those slim hands of hers slid up over his chest to link around his neck and she gave him a tender moan of pleasure as her tongue tangled with his. He held her close, loving the feel of her body pressed against him.

Eventually, she pulled back. Gazing up at him through those unforgettable eyes, she said, "I honestly can't stay all that long." Her no-nonsense tone only made him want to kiss her some more.

So he did.

Deep, endless kisses. Short, sweet, tender ones. Wet kisses, playful kisses. Kisses that felt to him like promises—the kind he feared she wasn't ready to hear or make or keep.

He was careful. He didn't push. She was the one who took his hand and led him to his bedroom. The kittens failed to follow. They were still busy chasing the jingle ball. He smiled against her lips as he shut the bedroom door with a nudge of his heel.

She unbuttoned his shirt as he walked her backward

to the bed. Laughing, she pushed the shirt off his shoulders. "I mean, I can stay a *little* while…"

"I am so glad to hear that." And then he kissed her again.

One kiss became another. They helped each other out of their clothes, dropping them to the bedside rug as they peeled them off. She was the one who paused to pull back the covers.

"Come down here," she whispered, catching his arm.

He went. They fell onto the white sheets together.

Happiness, he thought. *This is happiness.* Holding Kenzie. Kissing her. The happiness he'd known all those years ago. The happiness he'd left behind because of the terrible loss they'd suffered. Because at that time moving on had seemed more important than their young, wounded love.

He knew better now. He knew what really mattered. And this time, he wouldn't be throwing his happiness away.

"What is it?" She captured his face between her soft hands and looked up at him, frowning. "What's the matter?"

He put on a grin. "Not a thing. In fact, right now everything is pretty much perfect."

And he kissed her again, a long kiss, slow and sweet.

The doorbell rang.

Finn opened his eyes to the beautiful sight of Kenzie sound asleep on the other pillow. The room was dim, but the beginnings of daylight slipped through on either side of the heavy bedroom curtains. It was enough light to see by and he loved what he saw.

Kenzie slept curled on her side, facing him. He could feel the warmth of her, hear her soft, even breathing, make out the shape of her body beneath the blankets.

She was going to be freaked when she woke up. She'd meant to leave last night but he'd kept convincing her to stay.

"Just a little longer," he'd whispered at around 10:00 p.m. It couldn't have been much later that they both fell asleep.

He probably should be feeling guilty that he'd kept her with him overnight. But in fact, he was mighty pleased at the way things had turned out.

The doorbell rang again.

Kenzie stirred. "What's going on?" she asked sleepily. "What time is it?"

He rolled over to grab his phone from the nightstand. "Six ten a.m." He reached out and switched on the light.

She sat up with a gasp. "I stayed the night."

"And *I'm* glad you did—and I know, I know. You have to go." He pushed back the covers and swung his feet to the floor as the doorbell chimed for third time.

"Who's that?" she demanded.

He bent close and pressed a kiss to her forehead. "Not a clue. I'll go find out, though."

"And I'll get dressed and get moving." She blinked up at him owlishly. He just had to kiss her again. So he did, on that sweet mouth this time.

Gently, she pushed him away, then shoved her tangled hair back off her face and swung her bare legs to the floor. She wore nothing but a tiny frown. He looked her up and down slowly, taking in every lush, rounded inch.

"Finn?"

"Hmm?"

"The door?"

"Right…" He snatched his jeans off the floor, then pulled them on as she rose and started grabbing her own clothes. "Listen," he said, "you can leave the cats here. We'll hang out for a while and then I'll take them to your place."

She shot him a big, grateful smile. "They'll like that. Thanks."

"Anytime."

The doorbell jangled again—and then again. "Sheesh," she said. "Someone's impatient."

"They sure are."

"You think it's something serious?"

"Who knows?" He pulled open the bedroom door and found Tom and Ed sitting there, staring up at him. "Mornin', guys." He scooped them up, one in either hand. They purred in unison as he carried them with him to the front door.

When he got there, he set down the cats. They bounded off toward the kitchen. As the doorbell chimed again, he pulled the door wide.

His father stood on the other side. "It's about damn time," Finn Sr. said.

Chapter Nine

"What's going on, Dad?" Finn asked cautiously.

"You going to let me in? Coffee would be nice," Finn Sr. added with a look of pure annoyance.

Finn swallowed a sarcastic reply. Over the years, Finn had learned that getting snarky in return every time his dad gave him attitude never went anywhere good. He just let it roll off his back and saved his energy for the battles that mattered. Sadly, with his dad, there were always too many of those. "Sure. Come on in." His dad entered the house and Finn shut the door. "This way." He turned for the kitchen.

"Not a bad place," his dad said from behind him. "You ought to put in the effort to fix it up right, though. A man's home shows the world—"

"'The extent of his success.' I remember, Dad."

In the kitchen, Finn Sr. took a chair at the table. The silence was deafening as Finn got the coffee brewing.

At last, his dad spoke again. "So you have a cat now?" It was nothing short of an accusation.

Finn glanced over his shoulder to see Tom dart away into the great room. He smiled at the sight. "There are two. That one is Tom. They're not mine, though."

Kenzie appeared then, fully dressed, with Ed in her

arms. She paused in the large open arch to the dining room and great room. "They're mine," she said, and gave Ed a kiss on the top of his head. "How are you, Mr. Monahan?"

"Kenzie." Finn's dad actually blinked. "Kenzie Osborne."

"The one and only," she replied, nuzzling Ed, who purred loudly and nuzzled Kenzie right back. "It's…so nice to see you, Mr. Monahan." She said the words flatly, without a trace of warmth. And then she turned to Finn. "You sure about the cats?"

"Absolutely."

"Alright, then. I have to get going." She dipped to set Ed on the floor. He zipped off in the direction Tom had gone. Kenzie rose with remarkable grace considering how pregnant she was.

Finn went to her. "Drive carefully." He bent for a kiss.

She tipped her mouth up to him and smiled against his lips. "I will." And then she turned to his dad once more. "Have a nice visit, Mr. Monahan."

His dad regarded her coolly. "Please. We're all adults now. Call me Finn."

"Certainly." Icicles dripped from the single word. "Goodbye." She turned for the door.

"Be right back, Dad," Finn said flatly. He steeled himself for a rude remark.

But for once, Finn Sr. had the grace to keep his mouth shut. He granted Finn a curt nod.

"I'm sorry," Finn said quietly, when he caught up with Kenzie at the door. "I had no idea he would show up here."

"Don't be sorry," she spoke softly, for Finn's ears

alone. "He is who he is and that is in no way your fault." And then she kissed him. He felt the tension in his shoulders ease as she smiled against his lips.

A moment later, she was out the door. He watched her drive away and then returned to the kitchen, where his father was waiting.

"My God. Kenzie Osborne? And she's pregnant again, isn't she? I'm assuming it's yours…"

"No, Dad. It's not. But I wish it was."

"Well, whose is it then? Does she even—"

"Dad. Take a breath. Be very careful what you say next."

Finn Sr. blinked. But then he went right on talking. "What were you thinking to start in with her again? Why?"

Finn gave himself a slow count of ten before attempting a reply. Eventually, in a careful, even tone, he explained, "Because she's the best thing that ever happened to me. I blew it fifteen years ago and walked away from her. But I've grown up since then. Now, I know the value of what Kenzie and I had together and I want another chance with her."

"By God, Finn. You're making no sense at all."

"Wrong. *You're* not listening. But then, you never do."

"Please. You were eighteen with your whole life ahead of you. There is no reason for you to blame yourself for what happened then. That girl was holding you back and—"

"Kenzie never held me back." Finn made his voice ice-cold. "And please keep in mind that this is my house and you are a guest here."

His dad wore a look of infinite weariness. "Whatever

you say, Finn. And you're right. I didn't come here at six in the morning to talk about the, uh, past."

"Good." Finn went to the coffee maker, poured them each a cup and carried the cups to the table. "Just black, right?"

"Correct, thank you."

Finn took a seat, too. "Alright then. Whatever you came here to say, I'm listening."

"I told you via voicemail that we need to talk." His father scowled. "You didn't call back. And as it happens, I have a meeting in Billings, of all places. One of my top clients. I flew in there last night. And since it's only a couple of hours away, I got up at four and drove here. I have to be back in Tampa this afternoon, but I thought we could talk, that I could make you face what you really want. Make you get out there and create the career we both know you could have. You've got a chance in a million here. You could be the next—"

"Stop. Please. You said all that before. And I said that I like my life here in Montana and I have no interest in becoming a professional football coach. When a man tells you who he is and what he wants, believe him."

His dad groaned and slapped the table. "You're just afraid to fail again—and son, you *didn't* fail, not really. It was an injury that ruined everything. As a coach, you won't run that risk."

Finn took a moment to let all that sink in and found himself wondering, *Am I afraid?* Was that the real reason he didn't buy what his dad kept trying so hard to sell him?

No. It wasn't. Finn felt sure of that. "I am not afraid, Dad."

Blue eyes blazing, Finn Sr. leaned in. “Then what is it?”

“It's simple. I just don't want it, Dad. I don't know how many ways to tell you that I like who I am and I like what I do and I'm happy, right here in my hometown.” Tom chose that moment to leap onto his boot and attack it like a chew toy. “Come here, tough guy.” He scooped up the cat, gave him a quick cuddle and set him on his lap. Purring, the kitten tucked his paws and closed his eyes.

“I just can't get through to you,” his dad said angrily.

“Oh, you got through to me. I understand you perfectly. I just don't want what *you* want for me. I don't want to be like you. I'm not some eighteen-year-old kid who hasn't figured out what his life's about yet. I've been in the NFL. I've battled my way back from a serious injury—and then got injured again. Now I've chosen a new path for myself. And I like my path, Dad. I like it a lot.”

“What are you talking about? I only ever wanted the very best for you.”

“No. Uh-uh. You never tried to help me figure out what *I* wanted. You just pushed me without mercy to be what *you* wanted me to be.”

“Of course I did. Because you had what it took. Because you could have been the best of the best.”

“No. Wrong. It was all about you, Dad. About your son being an NFL superstar and how that reflected on you. At one time, I honestly believed I wanted the same thing you wanted. But now? Now I'm home, Dad. And I really like it here. I'm not going anywhere.”

“You're a fool, then.” His dad pushed back his chair and stood. “Or maybe you're not being honest with yourself. Are you sure you're not simply afraid to keep fighting, afraid to pull yourself together and do what it takes to make it to the top?" His dad glared down at him.

Finn met that glare without flinching. "You really are messed up, Dad. You know that? It's sad and it's painful. But I am not you. I am not a *reflection* of you. I have my own life and I like my life. A lot."

"I don't know what else to say to say to you." Finn Sr. glanced down at the expensive watch on his tanned wrist and added tightly, "I have a long drive and a plane to catch."

"Of course, you do. I'll walk you to the door."

Once the old man was gone, Finn fixed himself some breakfast. A little while later, he put the kittens in their carrier and took them to Kenzie's house.

That afternoon at practice, he felt kind of low. He kept remembering the crap his dad had laid on him, kept resurrecting childhood memories. As a kid, he'd tried so hard to please the unpleasable Finn Sr. Rarely had he made the grade.

He knew he shouldn't let his father get to him. But right now, Finn Sr. was definitely taking up space in his head.

At practice Barrett asked him if something was wrong. Finn played it off as exhaustion, said he'd been working long hours and felt kind of tired.

Later, in the parking lot, he found Kenzie waiting beside his truck, leaning back against it, her arms folded over her ever-expanding baby bump. "Okay," she said at the sight of him. "You need to follow me to my house. We'll talk about whatever went down with your dad."

He didn't want to talk about it. He just wanted to move on. "Aw, Kenz. I'm kind of beat."

"Oh, I bet you are. That man is a menace. Just being in the room with him for a minute wore *me* out. You need to follow me home." She gave him that look, the one that said there would be hell to pay if he didn't.

He gave in. Because he couldn't refuse her anything.

At her place, she poured him a stiff whiskey and soda. They sat in her living room by the fire, the cats cuddled on the sofa between them, and he gave her the play-by-play of his dad's visit.

Once he'd finished telling all, she said, "I honestly have no idea how your mother puts up with him."

"Was that a question?" he asked in a teasing voice.

"It was mostly hypothetical, but if you actually have an answer, please share."

He scratched Ed behind his little ear and chuckled when the kitten rolled to his back and wrapped all four paws around Finn's hand. As for Tom, he got up, yawned and jumped down from the sofa.

Finn tried to explain. "My mom's true-hearted. She sticks by her commitments through thick and thin. And it helps that my dad's always working. She really doesn't have to deal with him all that much. She's free to pursue good works and she does."

Kenzie made a thoughtful sound. "I remember she was always active in the community. She used to organize clothing and food drives."

"She still does. She's active in her church, too. Plus, she helps out at Covenant House and the Salvation Army. She's on the board of more than one charitable foundation and she donates a sizable chunk of the money my father makes to a long list of good causes."

"Wow. Your mom is a powerhouse."

"Oh, yes, she is."

"And she was always kind and sweet toward me." A soft smile curved Kenzie's beautiful mouth. "Even there at the end, when everything went so wrong that summer after high school."

"Yeah. She's the real deal. And I honestly think she loves my dad. He loves her right back. Don't ask me to explain it. I'm their son and I don't get it."

"They're just such a weird match," Kenzie said. "It's like if Glinda, the good witch, went and fell for Darth Vader." Finn's loud bark of laughter at that remark caused Ed to let go of his hand, leap up and dart off toward the kitchen. Then Kenzie added, "I'm glad you had your mom when you were growing up."

"Yeah, well. My brothers and I are in total agreement with you about that—and the truth is, Dad did put in time with us, my brothers and me. For me, he spared no expense when he saw I had what it took to make a go of it playing football. He sent me to clinics, made sure I had the best gear, showed up for every game. Yeah, it was a lot about him and how my success made him look good. And yet, he did pay attention. He gave me the support I needed to follow that dream."

"Too bad he's such a jerk."

"It is too bad. It really is."

Kenzie scooted closer, filling the space where the kittens had been. She leaned her head on his shoulder.

Finn curled an arm around her and kissed the top of her head. "I really am okay, you know."

She tipped back her head just enough to meet his eyes. "I'm glad." She raised those slim arms and wrapped them around his neck. He claimed another kiss. For an achingly sweet chain of minutes, they held each other close.

He loved what they'd found together since he moved back home. And he hoped that eventually she would see her way clear to giving him another chance—a *real* chance, the kind that lasted for the rest of their lives.

"What *are* you thinking?" She pressed her smooth palm to the side of his face.

You. I'm thinking of you and me. Of finally making it real after all these years, of building a life together, you, me and the baby…

"Not going to tell me, huh?" She didn't wait for an answer but instead got up and held her hand down to him. "Come on." He didn't budge, just stared up at her as his mind spun sweet fantasies of the future they could have together. "Finn…" She wiggled her fingers at him.

He took them. "Where are we going?"

"To bed."

He thought how fine she was, inside and out. "Now, that is an offer I cannot refuse."

"Well, then, get up. Let's go."

He rose and pulled her close. They shared one of those kisses that curled his toes and sent his pulse into overdrive.

"This way…" She took his hand again and led him to her room.

That Friday afternoon, the Titans boarded the bus for the hour-and-a-half drive to Buffalo Butte High, home of the Bulldogs.

It was a big deal, this game. The Titans hadn't played the Bulldogs in almost a decade. Why? The economy, of course.

During the rough times, people had pulled up stakes and moved on seeking somewhere they could make a living. That meant Tenacity High could no longer field a team large enough to play the Bulldogs.

But this year was different. The Titans were back, the energy high. Every player on the bus was pumped and ready to go. Finn had the realistic expectation that the team would bring home another win.

On the field, the Titans won the coin toss and chose to defer. The Bulldogs received the ball…and the Titans dominated from the start.

They started out strong, racking up two touchdowns in the first twelve minutes of play. Their kicker, Kevin Brown, came through with the extra point both times.

The crowd was at fever pitch. Then Remy O'Dare ran the ball to the end zone for a third touchdown and Kevin put the ball between the goalposts for a third time.

By halftime, the score was 35–3 in the Titans' favor.

But then in the opening play of the third quarter, the Bulldogs finally scored a touchdown and their kicker made that extra point. It was now 35–10. Finn's confidence remained high, though. They would win this game.

But six minutes into the third quarter, it all went to hell. The Titans' center, Skip Riley, snapped the ball to Remy, who executed a perfect pass to running back Sean Coolwater. Sean took off for the goal line.

He didn't make it. The biggest linebacker Finn had ever seen on a high-school football field caught up with Sean and brought him down. It was a brutal play. Finn thought he heard the sound of a bone snapping as Sean hit the ground.

When that linebacker got off him, Sean didn't move. The tackle had not only broken Sean's leg but knocked him unconscious as well.

Pulling her wheeled medical bag, Kenzie arrived at Sean's side a moment later. The Bulldogs' two trainers came running up, too. Sean regained consciousness quickly. But his leg did not look good. He'd suffered a compound tibial fracture.

The paramedics loaded Sean into the ambulance. They let his father ride with him to the hospital in Billings.

Having played the game for years and seen all kinds of ugly injuries, Finn knew that a compound fracture could take from four months to over a year to heal completely. Sean would most likely make a full recovery. But it would take time. He wouldn't be taking the field again this season.

The game went on.

But the Titans had lost both their spirit and the momentum. Finn did his best to get them back in the game, but it wasn't working. They never scored again.

The Bulldogs did, though. When the game clock ticked down to zero, the Bulldogs triumphed 43–35.

The bus ride home was way too quiet. Concern for Sean dragged the team down. And then, there was the loss they'd just suffered to the Bulldogs when for more than half the game, it had looked like they would get another win.

Finn played his part, reassuring them that Sean would recover fully and come back strong next year. As for losing a game they would so likely otherwise have won, Finn framed the loss as unfortunate and yet understandable, given the circumstances. Losses, he reminded them, were the best training there was for future wins. Just like Sean would in time, the Titans would come back strong—next game and the game after that.

Objectively, Finn thought he'd given a solid postgame talk. His players looked up at him, drinking in every word. Most of them nodded as he spoke. He was reaching them, at least. They seemed to have no clue that all his reassuring, supportive, hopeful words tasted like sawdust in his mouth.

At Tenacity High, he waited until all the players and staff had exited the bus and secured their rides home before heading for his crew cab. Kenzie was waiting for him there, her Bronco parked in the space next to his truck.

She came around the back of her SUV and straight for him. He almost broke down at the welcome sight of her rushing toward him. He reached out and she came into his arms, her hands sliding up over his shoulders, her arms wrapping good and tight around his neck.

"Hey..." He buried his face in the crook of her neck, breathed in her scent of citrus and vanilla, thought how much it meant to hold her close in his arms right now.

"Hey," she whispered back. They held each other tight right there under the glare of the parking-lot lights. When he loosened his grip on her a little, she pulled back enough to look up at him. "How're you doing?"

"I've been better."

"Sean will be alright." She said the words urgently.

He nodded down at her. "I believe you. It's just… recovering from an injury like that is no piece of cake."

"I know. But remember, you had an ACL tear. Those are tougher. Sean has better odds for a full recovery than you did."

"You sure about that?"

She reached up and gently brushed the short hair at his temple. "I am."

He kissed her again. How could he resist? And when he lifted his head, he managed a smile. "On a night like this one, I love that I've got you right here in my arms to remind me that everything is going to be okay."

"You're welcome. My place?"

He followed her home, where she led him to her room. They made slow, perfect love. Afterward, she dropped off to sleep.

Finn remained wide-awake. His mind was a hamster on a wheel, racing in circles, getting nowhere fast. He stared up at the dark ceiling above the bed and obsessed over the game, over all the ways he could have set things up for a better outcome, over everything he could have done differently so that Sean would not be lying in a hospital bed tonight, miles from home with a fractured leg.

He thought of the past, of his own injuries, of the end of his career in the NFL. Of how, for a while that had felt like a tragedy.

But it wasn't a tragedy. Far from it. Instead, it ended up being his chance for a new start, his chance to come home, to be here, in this bed, with this woman who had always been the only woman for him.

Closing his eyes in the darkness, he breathed in slow

and steady. He reminded himself that, in time, Sean would be fine. The boy would fully recover.

And as for Finn, he had everything he wanted right here in this bed with him.

Because Kenzie was here.

He smiled to himself. He loved Kenzie Osborne. And the time was coming for him to man up and tell her so.

Beside him, she stirred. Snuggling closer, she rested her hand over his heart. "It's not your fault," she said in a sleepy whisper. "It's football. There will be injuries."

"I know." He caught her fingers and brought them to his lips. "Go back to sleep."

"You too," she whispered.

"You got it." And then, he gathered her closer and shut his eyes.

Finn woke to daylight shining in on either side of the bedroom blinds. He turned to reach for Kenzie. But she wasn't there. In her place was an empty space and a dent in her pillow where she'd rested her head.

He heard a questioning meow from the other side of the shut bedroom door—and what was that smell? Coffee. Bacon… Breakfast, definitely.

He threw back the covers and reached for his pants.

When he opened the door, both kittens darted in. He scooped them up, one in either hand, and followed his nose to the kitchen, where he found Kenzie standing at the stove. Her back was to him. He took a minute to enjoy the sight.

She wore bib overalls and a white T-shirt. All that shiny hair was gathered into a single thick braid and tied with a bit of green ribbon. Her slim feet were bare and she had one hand at the small of her back.

As he watched, she rubbed the base of her spine, no doubt easing the ache from the weight of the baby. At this point, her pregnancy was obvious even from behind.

A strange blend of emotions rolled through him. Sadness for the baby they'd lost, joy for the little one she would hold in her arms before the year was out. Anger at that ex of hers for leaving her alone to raise their child without a dad.

And there was a sense of rightness, too—that he, Finn, would be here for her and for her baby the way he'd never had a chance to be for the child they had lost.

It was a good thing that he'd come home. And not just because he was happy here. Not just because he had a chance to make a life he would take pride in and a chance to contribute to the rebirth of the town he'd once left behind.

Most of all, he wanted a life with Kenzie. He saw that so clearly now. He wasn't a kid anymore, wasn't confused by his father's overbearing demands and his own need to somehow prove himself in a big, flashy way.

He knew what mattered now and he knew what he wanted.

Kenzie turned from the cooktop with a glowing smile. "There you are, sleepyhead."

"Mornin'." He set down the cats. They darted for the cat tree in the corner. It had scratching posts, padded shelves and a kitty lounge on the bottom level.

When he turned back to her, she was still smiling…at him. It was a smile that looked like happiness. Like she was honestly glad to find him there in her kitchen with her on a Saturday morning.

"Feeling a little better about things today?" she asked.

"Yeah." *Because of you*, he thought. "Thanks for putting up with me."

"Anytime." That look in her eyes? It was the same look she used to give him years ago—before they lost their baby, before he left her behind to chase his big dream. It was a look that said he was everything. That *they* were everything together. Because they were forever, Kenzie and Finn, and nothing and no one could tear them apart.

Yeah, he'd shattered her trust back then, stomped on it but good. And then she'd met Tate and got her heart blown to bits a second time. She'd made it crystal clear to him that she was done with love and romance, that she wouldn't try again with any man. She and her baby would be a family, the two of them.

But things could change, couldn't they? Broken trust could be rebuilt. He was not the messed-up kid he'd been back then. Surely, she could see that she could trust him now. He wasn't going anywhere. He would be here for both her and the baby. She could count on him now.

Was it possible that if he asked her now, she would agree to take a chance on him again?

"This is so good," he said a few minutes later when he sat across from her at the breakfast table. "Thank you."

"Enjoy." She gave him that smile, the one that made the world brighter.

They talked about last night's game. In daylight, the

loss didn't seem quite so hard to bear. There would be other games and the Titans would win again.

Top of mind for Finn was his injured player. "I want go visit Sean," he said.

Kenzie sipped her coffee. "He'll be hospitalized for a while, maybe a week, possibly longer. It's all going to depend on how he responds to treatment. You should wait a few days to drive out there. Your best bet is to call Sean's parents and say how much you'd like to go see him once Sean is ready for visitors."

A week, maybe longer? It wasn't a surprise, exactly. Finn knew from personal experience how tough the first days after a serious injury could be. Somehow, though, hearing Kenzie say the truth right out loud had him worried sick about Sean all over again.

"Don't do that," she commanded.

He regarded her warily. "Don't do what?"

"Don't start imagining the worst. Sean's at St. Vincent Regional. It's a level one trauma facility. They know what they're doing there. He's in good hands, believe me."

"Well, that's something, at least."

"Stop worrying. Check with the parents, find out how he's doing."

"Got it."

Finn would happily have hung around with Kenzie all day. But he had practice at ten and then real estate to sell in the afternoon.

Recovery practice was tough. Everyone felt low. Barrett led the team through a series of gentle stretches followed by light jogging, foam rolling and cold therapy. It fell to Finn to lead the game-film review and to talk about what they'd done right and what needed work. He kept it positive, focusing on new short-term goals, team unity and lessons learned.

Everyone wanted to know how Sean was doing. Finn reported that he'd called Sean's father before practice and learned that Sean had been through surgery. When he explained that Sean's prognosis was for a full recovery, everyone cheered.

"You can't visit yet," Finn told them. "For now, send get-well cards, gift cards for games and food, stuff that would cheer you up, stuff you would want if you were stuck in a bed recovering for a while."

After practice, Finn just wanted to head back to Kenzie's house, maybe stand at her door looking pathetic and emotionally needy until she took pity on his sorry ass and let him in. But no. He went right to work showing properties. His first appointment was only a few miles from town, but he had a 2:00 p.m. showing more than an hour away.

Once that second showing was over, he started to drive home. But ten miles down the highway on his way back to Tenacity, he slowed his crew cab, eased over onto the shoulder and pulled to a stop.

Staring off into the distance at miles of rolling prairie broken here and there by solitary rock formations and swathes of drift fencing, he made his decision. Life was too short. Anything could happen. He needed Kenzie to know how he felt and how much she meant to him.

He waited until the road was clear. Then he turned his crew cab around. Now he was headed for the larger town of Bronco and the upscale shopping area in what was known as Bronco Heights.

Once he got there, it didn't take him long to find Beaumont and Rossi's, a high-end jewelry store. An hour later, he came out with what he hoped was the perfect ring for Kenzie. It was not only absolutely beautiful, but also a ring she could wear on the job. The setting made it so she could pull on an exam glove without snagging. The ring had a round two-carat diamond in what the saleswoman called a low-profile bezel setting. The band was vintage gold. He thought it was gorgeous, that it was the ring she would choose over all the others. He sure hoped Kenzie would think so, too.

All the way back home, he argued with himself. She'd made it achingly clear she wouldn't be wearing any man's ring ever again.

But he couldn't help hoping, couldn't help wanting one more chance at a life with her. There was no way to get that chance except to ask for it…with all his heart and soul.

Back at his place, he paced the floor, muttering to himself, trying to come up with just the right words, the words that would dispel all her doubts and her fears. The words that would show her she was everything to him, that he would never let her down again, that he would always be there for her and for her little girl.

But nothing he could think of to say sounded right. Nothing sounded…good enough. Because come on. Why should she believe him, anyway? He'd let her down so completely before.

Plus, she'd said more than once that she wouldn't be marrying anyone ever again, that it would be her and her little girl, a family of two. Kenzie Osborne was a smart woman, a woman who knew what she wanted. He should probably believe her, take her at her word and accept that this, what they shared right now, was as good as it was going to get for them.

He paced the floor, feeling out of his depth, hoping against hope to summon the right words that would make her agree to give him one more shot at forever with her.

His phone chimed with a text…from Kenzie.

You hungry? I made chili. Come on over.

Chili. Kenzie made great chili. And then after dinner he could—

He froze in mid-step. What was the matter with him?

Was that his plan? Go to her place, chow down on her chili and then drop to one knee?

He was embarrassed that he'd even considered such a weak-ass move.

He should be putting together a grand gesture, taking her somewhere special, sweeping her off her feet, overwhelming her with the forethought and the attention to detail that went into setting the scene for the perfect proposal.

But when, exactly, could the two of them leave town for a romantic getaway?

They couldn't. Not in the next month or two.

And after that, she would be having her baby. By then, as she'd said more than once, their love affair would be over.

He really did need to make his move before they went back to being friends only, didn't he?

Hell if he knew. He *wanted* to make his move before she ended it. Once he was relegated to the friend zone he would be even less likely to get a yes out of her.

Wouldn't he?

Maybe a nice evening out. Say, dinner at Satterfield's…

And then what? Ask her to marry him over the crème brûlée?

He dropped to the sofa. His options in the near future were limited. And Satterfield's did sound better than at her place over chili.

He grabbed his phone and called her.

She picked up on the first ring and asked, "Are you on your way?"

His throat had locked up. He gave a ridiculous cough to clear the tightness and then asked, "How about I see if we can still get a table at Satterfield's?"

She laughed. "Tonight?"

"Well, uh, yeah…"

"What? You don't like my chili?"

He could hear the smile in her voice and knew she was teasing him."I love your chili. I just thought, you know…"

"What?"

"How about a nice Saturday night out for once?"

"Hmm…"

"Not in the mood for Satterfield's huh?"

"Hey. I'm in my third trimester. Last night, I drove to Buffalo Butte and back. While I was there, I irrigated, dressed and immobilized a compound tibial fracture. Then back here at home, the hottest guy I've ever known kept me up past my bedtime—and no, I'm not complaining that we stayed up late last night. It was worth it. But tonight, I just want to hang around the house and go to bed early, preferably with you." She laughed again, the throaty sound making him want to reach through the phone and gather her close.

She went on, "Right now, I'm in my old, ratty sweats and all I want is you, my kitties, a bowl of chili and maybe to check out what's on Hulu."

By then, he was smiling, too. "Twenty minutes, I'm there."

As soon as he walked in the door, Kenzie knew something was up.

For the next couple of hours, as they played with Tom and Ed, chowed down on chili and watched an ancient Clint Eastwood movie, she kept thinking, *Whatever it is, he's going to tell me any minute now.* But he didn't.

She kept catching him watching her, the strangest look on his face. As though he had something to say and was right on the verge of saying it—and then, at the last possible second, for some unknowable reason, he changed his mind.

Finally, after the movie and the popcorn, after the cats had curled up together in their bed by the fireplace, she couldn't stand it anymore.

They were sitting on the sofa. He had an arm around her. She'd drawn her legs up the side and put her head on his shoulder.

"Whatever it is you have on your mind," she said softly, tipping her face up to look in his eyes, "it can't be that bad. You should just tell me."

He kissed her, a light kiss, tender and so very sweet—and why was it that she just couldn't read him tonight?

He looked...worried, somehow. Even a little bit scared.

Finn Monahan never looked scared.

"Talk to me," she said, lifting her head to face him directly. Was he ill? Had he gotten bad news about Sean? "Finn. Please..."

He leaned close and kissed her. "Don't move. I'll be right back."

Without another word, he jumped up and headed for the door. She watched him reach into the pocket of his team jacket, which was hooked on the coatrack there. When he pulled his hand out, he had something in his fist.

She stared, bewildered, as he came back to her. When he reached her, he pushed the coffee table away from the sofa.

"What in the...?" She let the question die unfinished as he dropped to one knee in front of her.

That was when she saw that he held a black velvet box in his hand. Carefully, he lifted the lid and took out the most perfect ring she'd ever seen—antique gold with a beautiful, glittering round diamond rimmed in gold. A ring that seemed made just for her, the kind she could wear without fear it would get in the way while she took care of a patient.

Her heart pounded so hard she couldn't hear herself think. "Finn, I—"

"Marry me, Kenzie. Give me one more chance to be the man that you deserve. Let me take care of you and the baby. Let me be there for you. *With* you. For the rest of our lives. I know I messed up bad all those years ago, but I—"

"No."

He blinked. "What?"

"I, uh... Well, Finn, first of all, that's not true."

He looked so bewildered. "What's not true?"

"You didn't do anything bad all those years ago. We were so young. You didn't mess up. You were there for me, you stuck right by me until—"

"Don't try to sugarcoat it. I did mess up. You were everything to me and I left you, anyway." He held her gaze. "And I've always regretted that. Always wished I'd been a better man, a stronger man—and Kenzie, I *will* be better now, stronger now. I swear to you, I won't walk away, not ever again. I will always be right here beside you. I will be here for you and for the baby, if only you'll say yes." He took her hand then and he said, "Marry me, Kenzie. Be my wife."

She stared down at him, as her heart cried, *Yes! Yes, I will marry you, Finn. Just name the day!*

The truth was suddenly crystal clear to her. She could see it there, in his eyes. Feel it in her own tender heart.

She loved him, still, after all these years. And he loved her, too.

But their love wasn't what mattered. No.

Her baby was what mattered.

A child needed stability, needed a parent or parents she could count on. Looking at Finn now, knowing the strong, determined man he'd grown up to be…

She believed him. She trusted him to keep his word, to stay with her, never to walk away.

Yes, he'd left her before. But she honestly didn't blame him for leaving back then. He'd needed to go. And she'd needed more care and understanding than he could give her back then.

Now, though…

If she believed him now, married him, built a life

with him, gave her trust again completely, loved him with all her heart and then someday, as Tate had, he realized he wanted a fresh start and left her and her little girl behind…

No. She couldn't take that chance. Not now. Not with her baby's tender heart to consider.

Gently, she pulled her hand free of his hold. "I can't, Finn. I'm sorry. I meant what I said. I'm not getting married again."

He closed his eyes, drew a slow, shaky breath. "Just… think it over, won't you? Just give yourself time to—"

"No. Please believe me when I tell you my mind is made up and my choice won't change."

There was an awful, empty silence. Finally, he asked, "Are you sure?"

"Yes, I'm sure. I won't marry you, Finn. And I won't change my mind about that."

"Aw, Kenz…" He looked so sad, so…sorry, somehow. "You can't let yourself trust me, can you?"

She looked down at her tightly folded hands. "I'm so sorry. But you're right. I just can't."

There was a silence, several awful seconds of emptiness.

Finally, he spoke. "Fair enough." He returned that perfect ring to its little velvet box, swept to his feet and headed for the door.

When he got there, he put on his jacket and hat. Then, taking care to shut the door quietly behind him, he left. A minute later, she heard his crew cab start up and drive away.

Chapter Ten

It was so quiet once he was gone.

Kenzie sat there on the sofa for the longest time. Already, she missed him desperately. More than once, she grabbed her phone, started to call him, to beg him come back, to…

To what? There was nothing to come back for. She was not going to marry him. She'd learned the hardest lesson twice and she just couldn't take the chance of finding out if the third time might actually be the charm.

Yes, she'd hoped to keep his friendship. But who was she kidding? She cared for him deeply and he cared for her.

And yet, she couldn't say yes to him. There was nowhere for the two of them to go from here.

She got up, went to the kitchen and took a few tissues from the box on the counter. Back in the living room, she dried her eyes.

And when she looked down, Tom and Ed were sitting there at her feet, tails curled neatly around their front paws, staring up at her as though they weren't sure what to do.

She swiped away another tear before it could fall. And

then, she dropped to the sofa again and patted her lap with both hands. "Come on, guys."

They jumped to the sofa, climbed into her lap and started purring for all they were worth. She cuddled them, swallowed down the tears and longed for the man she couldn't let herself have.

Monday at lunch in the teacher's lounge, both Lauren and Sandy wanted to know what in the world had happened to Kenzie. Apparently, the breakup with Finn was written all over her face.

Lauren leaned close to her and whispered, "You've been crying. What happened?"

Kenzie straightened her shoulders. "I'm fine."

Sandy made a pouty face. "It's hurtful when you lie to us. What's going on?"

Kenzie pressed her lips together and shot a quick glance around the lounge. All the tables were taken. The last thing she needed was to share her heartbreak with the majority of her colleagues at Tenacity High.

Lauren suggested, "It's a nice day. Let's take our lunch outside."

Kenzie resisted, but her friends were relentless. The three of them ended up taking their bag lunches out to the athletic field, where they sat on the bleachers, Sandy and Lauren on either side of her. On the field, a girl's PE class practiced soccer drills.

"Talk," commanded Sandy as she took a bite of her ham on rye.

Kenzie had planned to keep her mouth shut, to stonewall her friends until they finally gave up. She really didn't want to talk about it—especially not at work.

But she looked in Sandy's worried eyes as Lauren leaned close and whispered, "Just tell us. You'll feel better."

"Finn and I broke up."

Dead silence. Both of her friends were shaking their heads.

Finally, Sandy asked the big question. "Why?"

Kenzie dropped her chicken-salad sandwich back onto the plastic wrap in her lap. "He asked me to marry him."

"And…" prompted Lauren.

"It's simple. I'm never getting married again."

"You turned him down?" said Sandy with a moan.

"That's right. I turned him down. He left. That was Saturday. I haven't talked to him since."

Her friends scooted closer. They each wrapped an arm around her. It helped. But only a little.

Lauren said, "Please don't call me a traitor, but—"

Kenzie leaned her head on Lauren's shoulder. "Never. You're the best."

"—Finn is one of the good ones," she continued. "And in my experience, the good ones are pretty darn hard to find."

"Call him," said Sandy. "Tell him you made a mistake and you need to talk and— Wait. I have to ask. Was there a ring?"

Lauren scoffed. "Please. It's not about the ring."

"I know," said Sandy staunchly. "But *was* there?" At Kenzie's slow nod, she demanded, "Okay, I'm going to need a description. A detailed description."

Kenzie sighed. "Fine. It was perfect. A gorgeous round diamond, antique gold band, low-profile, bezel-set."

"Oh, my…" Sandy shook her head. "That sounds like the exact right ring for you—and gorgeous, to boot."

"Yes, on both counts."

Sandy whimpered in distress. "I can't believe you turned him down."

"Oh, please," grumbled Lauren.

"Don't give me that look, Lauren," Sandy muttered in return. "I don't mean because of the ring—though let's be real, the perfect ring matters." She turned to Kenzie again. "I'm just shocked that you said no because you two were made for each other. I loved seeing you together. Finn's a great guy and you deserve the best."

"Stop now," said Lauren softly.

"Sorry." Sandy gave Kenzie's shoulders a gentle squeeze. "Sometimes I do get a little carried away."

"Nothing to be sorry about," Kenzie reassured her. "And you're right. Finn's a terrific guy. It's just that, after the disaster of my marriage to Tate, I don't want to get married again. I honestly don't. My baby needs a family she can count on absolutely. And that would be me, period."

"We are here for you," whispered Lauren.

"You bet we are," added Sandy.

Kenzie slipped an arm around each of them. "Thank you." They shared a group hug. Her friends were the best. And their support should have made her feel better.

But it didn't.

Later that afternoon, Kenzie took her place at the base of the bleachers for football practice. It was the first time she'd seen Finn since their breakup Saturday night.

He looked so good, so tall and strong and handsome. Her heart ached just to see him out there on the field putting the team through the usual drills. He didn't come near her.

Which was good, she reminded herself. They needed to avoid each other now. Distance would help them to move on.

But the pain of losing him just felt so…fresh.

It would get better, she promised herself. Eventually, the hurt would fade to a dull ache and then, over time, to nothing. After all, that's how it had been when it ended with Tate.

Finn is not Tate, said a stern voice in her head. *Finn's a good man and you know it. He's a man you can trust. He's the man that you love—and you're a fool to have sent him away.*

She blocked that voice out—or at least she tried to.

But she couldn't stop thinking about him, missing him, wondering what was he doing now?

The pain of missing him was bad. Really bad. And if it was going to feel this bad forever, she didn't know how she would bear it.

Tuesday morning, Finn got the okay to visit Sean at the hospital in Billings. He rearranged his work schedule and left home at ten.

At twelve thirty, he walked in on Sean just as an aide was taking away his lunch tray. The boy seemed glad to see him and in reasonably good spirits.

"It's going to be a lot of work and a long recovery," Sean said. "But I'm tough. I'll be back on the field next season. You can count on me, Coach."

Finn gave the boy a big smile. "Now, that's the best news I've heard all week. And I'm not the only one looking forward to having you back on the field. The whole team is on your side, Sean."

"Thanks, Coach. That's real good to hear."

Finn had brought DoorDash and Uber Eats gift cards so Sean could order whatever he was hungry for from a variety of Billings restaurants. He also gave Sean a ball autographed for him by all the other players on the team.

Sean said he'd gotten a lot of calls and an endless chain of texts. "It's good," he said. "To know the guys are rooting for me."

Finn stayed until a nurse entered the room to get Sean up on his crutches for a trip to the nurses' station and back.

In the car on the return drive to Tenacity, Finn opened the windows, cued up his favorite playlist and turned the volume up good and loud. Sean would be fine…eventually. Finn could let himself believe that now.

What he couldn't do was talk to Kenzie about it, tell her how brave Sean was, how good it felt to know the odds were solidly in Sean's favor for a complete recovery.

It hurt, plain and simple, that he couldn't reach out to her. So he tried to put her from his mind, tried not the think how empty his days felt without her in them.

That afternoon at practice, Kenzie kept a smile on her face.

It wasn't easy. In fact, it hurt more today to see Finn out there on the field than it had the afternoon before. It was supposed to get better, wasn't it? Or at least not get worse.

But it *was* worse. She missed him so much. It was fifteen years ago all over again, only more so. She ached for him. She needed him near.

Too bad that couldn't happen—because she'd sent him away.

She kept thinking about her talk with Lauren and Sandy the day before. They thought Finn was a great guy. Because he was. And knowing that just made the pain of losing him all the more unbearable.

She reminded herself that it had only been a few days. She needed to be patient. In time, she would feel better.

She was sitting on the bleachers, her medical bag ready at her side, watching Finn and Barrett lead the team through their usual preliminary warmup routine when Oscar appeared carrying a tray full of water bottles. He sat down next to her.

"Nurse Osborne," he said, staring straight ahead. "Something is wrong. It was wrong yesterday. You're not okay, are you?"

She drew her slumped shoulders back and gave him her warmest smile. "I'm okay, Oscar. I really am."

He slid her a quick glance and then looked away again. "I don't believe you," he said under his breath.

"Oh, Oscar…" She brushed his arm without stopping to think that he wasn't all that fond of random people putting their hands on him. "Sorry…"

He leaned toward her but kept his gaze on Finn and the team. "It's okay. But I still don't believe you. You look at him and he looks at you, but never at the same time anymore."

She didn't know what to say. Worse, her eyes had gone misty and her throat felt tight. She swallowed hard to force the tears down. "I just… Please don't worry, Oscar. It's going to be okay."

"Worry doesn't work that way," muttered Oscar. "You can't turn it off like a light." And then, he jumped up, grabbed his caddy of water bottles and headed onto the field.

Kenzie remained in her usual spot on the bottom row of bleacher seats. She couldn't help thinking that Oscar was right. She couldn't turn worry off at will any more than she could keep her thoughts from straying to the people she cared about.

No one needed medical attention that day, which gave her mind and her eyes way too much time to wander. Both her thoughts and her gaze kept straying to Finn. It didn't seem to matter how hard she tried not to think of him, not to look at him. The moment she let down her guard, her attention swung right back where it wanted to be.

She missed him desperately, so desperately that she had started thinking the impossible, that she really would try again with a man…if that man was Finn Monahan.

But that was just a fantasy, she reminded herself. Trusting a man wasn't possible for her. Not anymore. And Finn was partly to blame for that. Just because she understood why he'd left her all those years ago and actually believed it was the right thing to do at the time didn't mean she'd forgotten the awful pain of losing him.

At home alone in bed that night with Ed and Tom curled up together at her side, Kenzie thought about what Lauren had said a while ago now—that any man who made Lauren consider giving him her trust would have to be something special.

Finn was just that, something special. He was also a grown man now, a man who'd said he was ready to take care of her and her baby. She'd believed him when he said it.

But she'd held firm to her plan to raise her baby on her own, not to give her trust to him again no matter how many ways he proved he was worthy of it.

It had hurt so much to send him away. She'd known, though, that she'd done the right thing.

Too bad that since then, doubt had crept in.

Honestly, who was she kidding?

She loved him. Sometimes she couldn't help thinking that she'd loved him since he was hers in high school, that she'd lied to herself for fifteen years, even married another man. But what good had all that denial and a broken marriage to the wrong man done for her in the end?

No good at all. Because the whole time, she still loved Finn.

The hard truth was, she'd never stopped.

At practice the next day, the team seemed more determined, more cheerful. And more focused.

Finn got Barrett aside for a moment and asked him if he'd noticed the sudden change in the players.

"I've noticed," Barrett replied.

Finn regarded the other man sharply. "I'm getting the feeling you know what's going on here."

"I do, Coach." Barrett couldn't hide his grin.

"Tell me."

"Remy O'Dare, Darren Tuttle and Kevin Brown got permission to miss school today. The three of them drove to Billings and back."

Finn got the picture then. Three of the team's top players had made a special trip to St. Vincent Regional. "They visited Sean," he said.

"Yes, they did. And they came straight back to school from there. They got here about an hour ago. Evidently, the grapevine still works. Just about everyone at Tenacity High knows now that Sean is feeling good, already getting stronger and determined to reclaim his spot on the team next fall. The news is turning out to be a real spirit-lifter."

Finn scoffed. "I told them the same thing the other day after I went to visit him."

Barrett shrugged. "Apparently, it means more coming from their teammates."

Well, that was humbling. Finn muttered wryly, "Yeah. Probably so."

They got back to work. Practice went well.

Except for how hard it was not to keep checking the first row of the bleachers, keep stealing glances at the woman in the maroon scrubs and barn jacket, her silvery gold hair in that heavy braid down her back.

Damn, she was beautiful. And he couldn't stop wishing that something would change, that he would find a way to earn her trust again, that somehow, he still might make her his.

Finn was the last to leave the field after practice. When he got to his crew cab, he found Oscar waiting by the driver's door.

"Hey, Oscar." Finn forced a smile. "Need a ride home?"

"Thanks, Coach. But my dad will take me." Oscar tipped his head toward the pickup waiting two rows away.

Jesse Abernathy sat behind the wheel. He waved out the open driver's-door window and Finn waved back.

Finn stuck his hands in the pockets of his team jacket and leaned back against his crew cab. "So what's going on?"

Oscar mirrored him, hands in his pockets, eyes on the sky. "You're a good coach. I like working with you."

So…this was a testimonial? That seemed unlike Oscar. It was just too…touchy-feely. Oscar wasn't much for emotional declarations of respect and admiration.

"Thank you, Oscar," Finn replied. "We're lucky to have you on staff."

Oscar let out a hard huff of breath. "You're a good coach. But you're not so smart about some other things."

Finn replied cautiously, "Like what?"

"You're not happy. Nurse Osborne isn't happy. Something went wrong for you guys."

Finn had no clue how to respond. No way should he be discussing his feelings for Kenzie with a student. "Oscar, I—"

The boy put up a hand. "Not finished, Coach."

"Uh, okay…"

"It all seems so simple. Being happy is better. Just tell her you love her. How hard can that be?"

"I—"

"That's all." Oscar opened and closed his hand. "Sometimes I just need to say what I'm thinking. You have a good night, Coach." And with that, he turned on his heel and took off for the pickup waiting two rows away.

Finn watched him jog over there, heard the pickup door open and shut as the boy got in on the far side. Jesse waved again. Finn raised his hand in a slow salute as they drove by him. Then, for several minutes after that pickup had vanished from sight, Finn stared up at the star-thick sky and thought about what Oscar had said to him.

That night, Finn hardly slept at all. He kept seeing Kenzie's beautiful face, the sadness in her eyes when he'd asked her to marry him.

The next morning he woke up exhausted. Even after three cups of coffee he still felt like crap. And the day ahead? Packed, as usual. He showed houses from nine to three.

At practice it was harder than ever not to constantly glance Kenzie's way. More than once, she just happened to be looking at him when his gaze strayed to her.

It was heaven, that jolt of awareness when their eyes met.

It was also hell. He wanted to stare at her forever, but instead he made himself tear his gaze away. A few minutes later, he would sneak another look at her. Sometimes she was looking right back.

And sometimes she was staring anywhere but at him.

Three or four times his focus landed on Oscar, who either looked away like Kenzie did, or glared at him. Apparently, Oscar was getting pretty fed up with him at this point.

And Finn couldn't blame the kid.

Oscar was right. Finn was miserable. And being happy was definitely preferable to the gray funk that served as his constant companion since Kenzie had turned him down five days ago.

Just tell her you love her.

Easy for Oscar to say. If Finn dared to try again, she

would only turn him down a second time. He had no desire to beg for another rejection.

But how could getting turned down a second time be worse than not trying at all? At least if he tried again, he would have the consolation of knowing he'd done the best that he could.

Because the more he thought about the situation, the more he had to admit that Oscar was right—and not only about happiness being preferable to misery.

Last Saturday, Finn had failed to say the most important words. He'd gotten so wrapped up in telling her all that he would do for her that he'd totally forgotten to share what was in his heart.

Talk about an unforced error. He might not win her love by trying again. But at least he would get a second chance to say the words that mattered most.

He lingered after practice, hanging around in the gym until everyone had cleared out. A few minutes after that, he found himself standing in the empty parking lot alone, thinking about calling her, just whipping out his phone and asking her if she would let him come over.

He did pull the phone from his pocket. But he couldn't quite work up the nerve to hit the call icon. He drove home instead.

At his house, he brought up her contact again. And then he stood there by the kitchen island staring at her name, longing to hit *call*—but balking because if she said she didn't want to see him, he would be done before he started. Finally, after twenty minutes of waffling, he stuck the ring box in his jacket pocket, climbed back into his truck and returned to town.

The lights were on at her house. He parked at the curb, got out and marched up the front walk to the door.

When she pulled the door open, his heart stopped. Her hair was loose on her shoulders and she'd changed into joggers and a giant sweatshirt with Underestimate Me… That'll Be Fun printed across her chest above the giant roundness of her baby bump.

He'd never seen anything so beautiful in his life as Kenzie standing in that open doorway, the light behind her creating a halo around all that white-gold hair.

"Hi," he said, because he hadn't summoned the forethought to think of something better. "Can I…come in?"

She studied his face. He waited for her to say *Finn* in a regretful, why-are-you-here? kind of way—or even go so far as to shut the door on him.

But a miracle happened. She stepped back and gestured him forward. He was over that threshold in an instant. She shut the door behind him as both Tom and Ed darted in from the dining room.

"Hey, guys." They came right for him. He bent and scooped them up. Ed purred in his left ear, Tom in his right.

All of a sudden, he felt better about everything. Because, hey. She'd shut the door with him on the inside of it. And at least Tom and Ed seemed glad to see him.

As for Kenzie, who could tell? She just stood there watching him through wary eyes, no doubt waiting for him to get on with whatever he'd come here for.

Crouching, he released the kittens. They bounded off through the arch that led to Kenzie's home office and the stairs.

He tried to think of a really good opening line. Too

bad his mind was blank as a sheet of white paper. He hadn't prepared and he felt like the fool he was.

Kenzie took pity on him then. "Coffee?"

"No."

"Then…?"

"I need to tell you…"

"What?"

"That I…love you. Only you. That there was never anyone but you, not really, not in my heart."

She gulped. "You mean that?"

"I do. I always did. I always will. Kenzie, I loved you so much way back then—loved you more than anything. I never should have left you."

She took a step closer, laid her smooth hand against his cheek. His whole body burned at that touch. "That was then. Forget about then. It's gone. Let's just talk about now."

He caught that soft hand of hers and pressed a kiss into the center of her palm. "All the things I said last Saturday morning, I meant them, all of them. I want you and I want the baby. I want what I walked away from all those years ago—a life with you, the forever kind. I want a home with you, a future with you *and* with the baby—hell, with Tom and Ed, too… All of it. I want more kids later if that works for you. We can talk about that—I mean, if any of it is even possible, if you think that you might just maybe be able to love me, too."

"Oh, Finn…"

He was still on his feet. Should he be on his feet?

No, he should not.

He dropped to one knee right there in front of her, then

swept off his hat and pressed it to his heart. But it was just in the way there, so he tossed it over his shoulder.

She stifled a laugh. "Finn, what in the…?"

"Kenzie." He still had her hand, so he pressed his lips to it. And then he said, "I am so in love with you I can't see straight. The truth is, I always have been, ever since that first day I walked you home freshman year. I was in love with you when we were fourteen and I never stopped. And Kenzie, if you can see your way clear to giving me one more chance, I swear on my life, on all that I hold dear, that I will never let you down again."

Kenzie swallowed. Hard. "Finn?"

"Yeah?"

"Oh, Finn." A tear slid down her cheek. "I love you, too."

"Kenz. Please don't cry…" He swept to his feet and gathered her into his arms.

And then they were kissing, deep and slow and oh, so tenderly.

When he finally lifted his head, he said in a rough growl, "Make me the happiest guy on the planet. Marry me, Kenzie."

She blinked away more tears and nodded. "I will, yes. I love you, Finn. So very much. I've missed you so much since I sent you away. I'm so glad you're here, so glad you didn't let me chase you away."

He drew a slow, ragged breath. "You mean that?"

"With all my heart."

"Damn. I was scared to death you'd just say no again."

"No way. The past five days without you have been hell. I love you, Finn Monahan. You're the one for me. And yes, I will marry you."

He kissed her again, claiming those sweet lips for the longest time. He could have gone on kissing her forever, but there was one more thing he had to do first. Carefully, he slipped the black velvet box from his pocket and took the ring out.

With a shy smile, she gave him her hand. He slid that ring on her finger. "It fits," he whispered in relief and pure joy. He kissed the back of her hand. "I took a guess about the size."

She stared down at it with a sigh. "It's perfect. I love it so much. And I love you."

And then they were kissing again, holding on tight to each other as he guided her backward to the short hallway that led to her room.

He started undressing her before they'd even reached the bedroom. She returned the favor. In no time, they were both wearing nothing but happy smiles.

They stood by the bed, their arms around each other.

"Let's make it soon," she said, and kissed him hard and quick. "I want to be married to you. We've wasted too many years already."

"Yes," he agreed. "Soon is great. I can't wait, either. It's about damn time."

She kissed the scar on the bridge of his nose. "Nothing fancy. A few friends, my mother if she can make it. My dad, too. Your mom and dad and your brothers…"

"I'll invite them. But, well, you know my dad. He's usually nothing but trouble in an endless list of ways."

"We'll deal with him. He doesn't scare me."

"Okay, we'll invite him, too," Finn replied and then added, "But if my family can't make it, I don't want to wait for them. I want you to be my wife and I want that before the baby comes."

"Yes," she said, holding his face between her hands, pressing her forehead to his. "Yes…"

"I like your house," he added after another endless, searching kiss. "I'm thinking we could sell mine. Is that okay, if we live here?"

"Of course." She looked up at him, those beautiful eyes shining. "I would like that, too."

"What else do we need to talk about?"

"Right now, not a thing," she said with a wicked smile. "Right now, we're going to consummate this union of ours."

"That is an excellent idea." He scooped her high in his arms, then carried her the rest of the way to her bed.

That Friday night, the Titans played the White Rock Coyotes at home.

The Titans were confident, ready to go. Oscar Abernathy felt the energy on the field and knew that the team would come back strong from last week's defeat.

And they did. When the game clock ticked down to zero it was Titans 30, Coyotes 13.

And the Titans' victory wasn't the only good news that night. Everyone was talking about Coach Monahan and Nurse Osborne. She wore Coach's ring on her finger.

Oscar wasn't the least surprised to learn that Coach and Nurse Osborne were getting married. Coach was no fool.

He'd just needed a little nudge in the right direction.

* * * * *